You Were Mine at Merlot

A LOVE IN WINE COUNTRY NOVEL

PAMELA GIBSON

Edited by Faith Freewoman and Mark Gibson

Cover Photo from Shutterstock
ISBN 978-0-9976885-0-4
Manufactured in the United States of America
First Edition July 2016

To my nieces, Maria Dicken and
Meredith Krauss,
who suggested this title.

Chapter 1

Love all, trust a few, do wrong to none.
--William Shakespeare

Empty wine bottles stood like tired soldiers amid a battlefield of crumpled napkins, dirty plates, and curling rose petals. The ice sculpture dripped water into its holder and crumbs littered the floor near the cake table.

Mariel Reynoso surveyed the mess with a satisfied smile.

The party had been perfect.

She set the cleaning crew to work and strolled across the parking lot to her car. She loved engagement parties.

Maybe I'll get to plan my own someday.

Nice sentiment, but she doubted it. Lately, her choice of boyfriends had been as thrilling as a free fall down a rocky slope.

The face of her ex intruded. Lane was a good example of what happened when you let your ego crowd out good sense. He was an actor in a popular television series filmed in Napa, and she'd been dazzled by his attention. He also had star-sized issues.

He's out of my life now.

Was he? Their last conversation had been unsettling. He insisted he wanted her back and would not take no for an answer, but she was sure he wasn't heartbroken. He just couldn't stand the thought that he'd been the one dumped. It wasn't good for his image.

What I need is a big, brawny boyfriend to convince him I've moved on.

But where would she find one? She was so busy she didn't have time for a social life.

Mariel pulled out of the driveway, stuck her hand out the window, and let cool air glide over her fingers. The summer night was crisp, and the sky so clear she could almost count the stars spread over her like a glittering canopy.

Tonight *she* was a star.

Planning events at La Golondrina Winery was fun and paid the bills. The best part was that she might be in line for a promotion at the end of summer. The marketing director was retiring. Her job took her all over the country setting up winemaker dinners in prominent restaurants to showcase their wines. It had huge responsibilities and a big salary.

If she got it, she'd be just as important as her sisters.

She smiled, thinking about how skeptical her parents had been when she told them she'd accepted a job in a winery and would not be transferring to a four-year school when she finished junior college.

"Why are you leaving school? Can you not get serious about your future? You want to pour wine and plan parties? Oh, Mariel..."

"Oh, Mariel" seemed to be her mother's mantra. Because she was the youngest, her parents thought she needed help making decisions. They meant well, and she loved them, but they tended to interfere, wanting her to be more like her two older siblings. Paige and Lindsay were college graduates. They were organized and methodical and had successful careers. She was creative and impulsive and was still feeling her way into the future.

She needed to step out of their shadows. If she worked hard, she'd get the promotion and finally do it.

A flicker of doubt made her tighten her hold on the steering wheel. Others had applied for the job. Could she compete?

Of course I can. It's June, it's wedding season, and it's my time to shine.

Her smile was wide as she slowed for a curve. The road that went up valley and over the mountain could be treacherous at night if you didn't know the hairpin turns. She'd traveled the difficult road so many times over the past three months, she'd decided to move closer to work when her lease was up in her St. Helena condo.

Headlights loomed in her rearview mirror, but Mariel couldn't get over to let the car pass. Too many curves ahead.

The car crept up and camped on her bumper.

"Really?"

She speeded up. The car stayed with her. Its bright lights blinded her whenever she looked in the mirror.

What an idiot! Doesn't he know I can't pull over? Jeez. Give a girl a break.

She resumed her safe speed, but couldn't shake the chill that crept between her shoulder blades. She rolled up the windows and made sure the automatic door locks were engaged.

A road sign flashed by in the dark—a double passing lane was ahead. When she reached it she moved into the right lane, slowed, and waited for the car to pass. It didn't. It moved in closer behind her.

Could something be wrong with her car? Several people were in the parking lot when she drove away, and no one motioned to stop her.

Her palms were damp and she was breathing so fast she was getting lightheaded. Don't panic.

The passing lane ended and both she and the tailgater

merged back onto the two-lane road. A car coming from the opposite direction temporarily blinded her, but passed quickly.

Enough!

She stopped on the shoulder of the road, expecting the car behind to zoom past. It didn't. It parked behind her and the headlights went off.

Maybe there was an innocent explanation. Maybe there was an urgent message for her, although she couldn't imagine what it could be.

Thick trees lined both sides of the road and her instincts told her to keep her car running and her lights on. She clutched the steering wheel like it was a life preserver. Maybe this wasn't such a good idea.

Moonlight was dim. She peered out her window and saw a short, husky man approach. She swallowed hard and yanked the door open, ready to confront the asshole. Too late she noticed his face was covered.

A ski mask?

Her heart pounded in her ears. She slammed and locked the door and sped away, her chest tight, her nerves in knots.

Near the summit, she scanned the road ahead for a house with its lights on. Not a pinprick showed through the dense trees. She grabbed her purse with one hand and sifted through it for her cell phone. Her fingers closed around it, but it slipped onto the floor. Crap. The other car was behind her again. She didn't dare stop to find her phone.

The front bumper of the car behind nudged hers. Stifling a scream, she tried to focus on the road. Her brain was numb, right when she needed to be alert. Someone she knew must live on this road.

Keira Leoni.

They'd been friends in school, and Mariel had been a frequent visitor, doing homework and helping her harass her older brother. She hadn't been to the house since Keira left for college, but this was an emergency, and the driveway was a short distance past the summit.

Please let the Leonis be home.

The tailgater inched closer and moved alongside, as if trying to force her off the road. She knew there were steep drop-offs, but couldn't remember where they were.

Oh God, oh God.

She wasn't sure she could hang on much longer. If she speeded up, she could lose control of the car on the turns. If she slowed down, the follower could cut in front of her and force her to stop.

The Leoni's driveway was just around the curve. She had no choice now. She made a hard right into the drive and stopped in front of the darkened porch. The other car followed and parked in the center of the narrow drive, blocking any escape.

Her would-be assailant leaped out of the car and

yanked on her locked door. She screamed and pumped the horn.

The porch light flicked on and the front door of the house opened. The dark figure bounded away from Mariel's car and ran back to his vehicle. Tires sprayed gravel when the car backed out and sped off.

A bare-chested man with immense shoulders and clad in pajama bottoms came up and knocked on her window. His face was in shadow, but the build was not that of Keira's father.

Crap, I got the wrong house. Maybe this guy would be worse than the man who ran off. Tears trickled down her cheeks.

"Are you all right?"

Her throat was so tight she couldn't respond.

"Unlock the door," said the deep male voice.

She was frozen to the seat.

"Nobody's going to hurt you. You can open the door."

His tone was familiar and compelled her to comply. Maybe the adrenaline had worn off. The fight was suddenly gone from her body.

Strong arms reached around to unbuckle her seat belt.

"Can you stand?"

Why wouldn't she be able to stand?

She stepped out of the car and immediately fell to her knees. He reached down, lifted her into his arms, and kicked the car door shut.

She couldn't think. Her breaths were coming in rapid, shallow gasps. She gulped a few times, but there wasn't enough air. She began to pant, the warmth of the hard-muscled chest against her cheek her only reality.

And then the world faded away.

* * *

Zack Leoni looked at the woman on his couch. He checked her breathing and situated her with pillows under her feet. Then he unfolded his mother's plaid throw and covered her gently to make sure she stayed warm.

What was that all about? Lovers' spat? Attempted robbery? Answers would come when she woke up.

Mariel Reynoso. Good thing she'd passed out. When she woke up and figured out who'd carried her in, she'd bolt for the door.

He sat back and let his gaze drift over her face and body. She'd been pretty as a teen-ager, if a little on the plump side. Her curves were still generous, but they were in all the right places, making her even sexier than she'd been the last time he saw her.

Five years ago at the infamous talent show.

He shifted in his chair. Guilt still plagued him.

She was wearing a low-cut, lacy black sheath with a string of pearls, like she'd come from a party. Long, black, slightly curled hair spread out down her back and over her shoulders. The soft hair smelled like coconut and had tickled his nose as he carried her in. And that body…it was enough to make him think about a cold shower.

And it wouldn't be the first time.

He went into the bedroom to pull on a pair of jeans and flannel shirt. No need to advertise his lustful thoughts. When he came out again, her eyes were open, but she hadn't moved. He knelt down next to her and picked up one of her cold hands.

"Hi. Remember me? Keira's brother?" Well, that was lame. Of course she remembered him, although she'd probably tried to forget him. "I don't know what was going on in my driveway, but I'm glad I was home. Can you sit up? I'll get you a glass of water."

There was no answer, but her beautiful green eyes widened and her bottom lip trembled. He felt pressure on his hand where it still held hers.

She must still be numb from her experience, or she definitely would not be holding my hand.

He lifted her head and gently slid a pillow underneath, careful not to tangle her hair.

"Are you warmer now?"

She nodded slightly, her eyes closing again.

He went into the kitchen and returned with a glass of water.

"Do you want to tell me what happened?" Zack's tone

was patient, the one he used with crime victims.

She shuddered and tears leaked out of the corners of her eyes.

"You're safe here, Mariel. Take a few deep breaths. Try to relax your shoulders."

He sat back and watched her face, steeling himself for what was coming. He saw the changes in her expression as his words—and his identity—finally registered.

She threw off the blanket and struggled to get up, mascara streaking down her cheeks.

"Oh, my God, I can't believe you're the one who rescued me. I'm out of here."

He stood to his full six foot three inches and pointed his finger at the couch. "Sit down, Mariel. I'm not letting you leave until you answer a few questions. Then I'm going to call this in."

Her eyes narrowed to slits and she sat, wiping her cheeks on the edge of the blanket.

"You mean call the cops?"

Zack sat on the ottoman in front of her and picked up the iPad lying on the end table.

"I guess you haven't heard. I'm back at the sheriff's department. I *am* a cop."

Chapter 2

Trust everybody, but cut the cards.
--Finley Peter Dunne

She didn't want to relive the experience. She wanted to go home. But he was still there...waiting, the tablet propped on his knees. His warm brown eyes radiated concern, and his face was set in a bland expression that was probably meant to reassure people. Dark hair that looked black in the shadows was worn short except in front. He pushed it back off his forehead and shifted his lean, muscular frame on the ottoman.

Zack Leoni.

Years ago he could make her laugh, and more than anything else right now, she needed to laugh...at herself, the situation, the horror. Laughter made anxiety recede, and she desperately needed the last half hour to go far, far away.

Anger worked equally well…anger that bubbled up from somewhere deep inside, where it had simmered for years, anger at herself for being stupid and naïve, thinking he cared—anger at him for rejecting her and leaving her to face the consequences.

"Are you feeling better?"

She fumbled in her purse for a tissue, dabbing at her eyes and face. "I really need to get home."

His solid body blocked her view of the fireplace, but she could hear it hissing and crackling, the sounds somehow soothing in spite of her agitation He looked at her as if assessing whether or not she really was all right.

Mariel folded her arms and glared, using fury to cover her fear. Someone had tried to run her off the road tonight. Why? She didn't have enemies. The thought brought the night's events roaring back, and terror took control of her muscles, making them taut and painful. She shuddered and to her disgust, tears trickled down her cheeks again.

He put down the tablet, picked up the throw that had fallen on the floor, and tucked it around her shoulders. A clean scent, like Ivory soap, surrounded her when he reached behind. His touch was gentle. It spoke of caring and concern. Deputy Sheriff, huh.

She took a deep breath and brought herself under control. This was his parents' house. Was he living here?

Her cousin Sam recently mentioned Zack had completed his tour of active duty in the Army, but it never occurred to her that he'd come back here to live.

She'd vowed their paths would never cross after what he did to her.

Don't you mean what you did to yourself? Isn't that why it still rankles after all these years?

It had been an impulsive act, one she regretted immediately. Memories rose…the charity talent show, the week of rehearsals, her constant flirtation with her cousin's best friend. Her crush on Zack had blossomed when he came home on leave from the Army and offered to help her cousin Sam backstage at the show.

Dressed in her sexy flamenco outfit, waiting at the edge of the stage for her cue, she'd stroked his cheek, gazed into his eyes, and boldly invited him to take her home after the show, telling him she had the house to herself and he could stay. Sam had dashed backstage, his finger pointing at the sensitive microphones in the ceiling. They were live, and the entire audience had heard her.

They also heard his rude rejection.

She'd run out of the auditorium, compounding her humiliation by skipping out on her act. Her emotions had taken charge, her face burning while she fled, her heart banging in her chest. She'd driven straight to her sister's empty cottage and buried her face in the fur of

Paige's dog, grateful that her sister was out of town and had left her in charge of both house and Bay, her yellow lab.

Now she glanced around the rustic living room. Its overstuffed chair and small couch faced a rock fireplace set into the wall. She hadn't been here in years, and couldn't remember details. But this room had masculine touches she was sure weren't there before.

Zack handed her the unfinished water and urged her to take another sip.

"I could brew some coffee or tea. Just say the word." He took his seat on the ottoman again. "Can you talk now?"

Mariel took a deep breath. Her embarrassment at being in Zack's presence warred with the comfort of knowing her ordeal was over. She really didn't want to be here, but she understood his need for details. Zack wasn't being polite. He was doing his job.

"You saw what happened. I don't have anything to add."

Zack's eyebrows rose. "Are you sure you're Mariel Reynoso? That chatterbox friend of Keira's who used to bug me when I was trying to do homework? The one who emptied the frogs out of my terrarium because they needed to be free?"

She remembered that day. She'd done it to get his attention.

"That Mariel never lacked conversation," he said. "She was always babbling. And dancing. Do you still dance?"

"Yes." She sighed. "Are we through?"

A slow smile spread across his gorgeous face, revealing perfect teeth. A tiny flutter dusted the inside of her stomach. *Damn.* He could still make her curl up into a warm ball. She forced her errant thoughts back to the events of the evening.

His smile faded. "Why don't you start at the beginning and tell me what happened, step by step?" He was all business now, and the sooner she got this over with, the sooner she could go.

"I was on my way home and a car camped on my bumper." She paused to take a sip of the water. "I slowed down to let him pass, and he slowed down. Then I speeded up, and he speeded up. When I pulled over to let him pass, he stopped and walked toward me. That's when I saw he was wearing a ski mask. I drove away as fast as I could."

Her hand shook, so she handed him the glass. He put it down and put his hand over hers. It was warm and firm.

She snatched hers away.

"Then I remembered your parents live up here. That's why I turned into this driveway."

He sat back. "My parents moved to Oregon about six months ago to be closer to Keira. My dad had a mild stroke, and my mom needs help caring for him until he gets better. I'm renting the house from them until they get some of their medical bills paid. You're lucky I was off duty and happened to be home."

She folded her hands in her lap. Keira had stayed in Oregon after graduating from college, but Mariel hadn't heard about the parents' move. Or his father's stroke.

"Where were you coming from?"

She looked up. "I had a party in Sonoma. I'm an event planner for a winery there."

"Did you have a fight with anyone at the party? Did you recognize anything about the person or the car?"

"No."

"Did you have a fight with your boyfriend?"

"I don't have a boyfriend."

"Now that's hard to believe." His expression was warm and firelight danced in his eyes. The flutter intensified. She was furious at herself for responding.

He set the tablet down. "If it's any consolation, there's been a guy targeting women on lonely roads at night. It probably has nothing to do with you personally. I'll call this in right now and tomorrow we can go over to the sheriff's substation together and fill out the paperwork." He studied her face as if waiting for a reaction. "If you're feeling better, I'll take you home now."

Mariel clenched her hands on the blanket in front of her. "I can drive myself home."

"Really? You want to take the chance the guy is still out there, waiting around a corner?"

He had a point.

"Where do you live now?"

"St. Helena."

He cocked his head. "Why did you take this road? I know the main highway between Napa and Sonoma is being worked on at night, but you could have gone up valley to a direct route over to Calistoga, then down Highway 29 to St. Helena on a better road."

She sank her teeth into her bottom lip. "I don't like that road. Paige's ex-boyfriend had an accident there and died, and it creeps me out when I drive it at night."

He shook his head. "When we're through tomorrow, we'll stop here and you can pick up your car and drive home. In the daylight. And you don't ever have to see me again."

"Well that's a relief." She tried for a haughty tone, but she felt a smile tugging at the corners of her mouth.

His offer made sense, even though she couldn't imagine being in a car with him all the way to St. Helena.

Mariel slipped on her shoes while Zack went into the other room and made his call. When he came back, he held out a large coat and helped her put it on. It reached practically to her knees and had his scent, which was oddly comforting.

"Ready?"

Mariel was amazed that she trusted Zack so completely, this man who was part of her public humiliation. And that was one of her other faults, according to her family. *"You're too gullible, too trusting, that's why you get into so much trouble, Mariel…"*

Zack was a cop. But it was more…he had a calm assurance, a confident, take-charge attitude, and he touched her so carefully, as though she were made of fragile glass.

Maybe he still feels guilty about his very public rejection.

The story was still alive. Tactless friends refused to let it die. Apparently it was too juicy to resist.

Mariel stopped to get her purse out of her car and followed Zack into a one-car garage. Inside was a late model gray sedan, something solid and practical. In the corner was a Harley-Davidson motorcycle.

That's more like the Zack I remember.

Silence was thick and no longer comforting as they drove down the dark road. What would have happened to her if he hadn't come out?

She trembled under the large coat, and to her mortification a sob escaped. She wasn't usually such a wimp, but this experience had freaked her out.

"Hey, you're okay, Mariel. You need to put this out of your mind. It's going to be hard, but you can do it. Will you try?"

His voice was soothing as he touched her hand. He knew better than to leave it there, but even a soft pat made her warm to her toes. She was furious that he could still affect her, but maybe it was only because her defenses were down.

"What time can you go in tomorrow?" she asked.

"We can go anytime. I'm...on vacation."

She heard the hesitation in his voice and turned to look at his profile, sensing tautness in his jaw, even though she couldn't see him clearly in the dark.

"Although I didn't get a good look at the plates, I can describe the car and the body type and height of the perp," he said. "I expect you saw even less. People who are terrorized don't often remember details. It feels better to block the memories."

He was right. All she wanted to do was forget, but she knew it would be a long time before the experience faded.

When they reached her condo, Zack got out and opened her door, holding her arm while they walked to the front door. She still felt a little wobbly, but wasn't sure if it was her bad experience or the proximity of the man next to her. Finding her key, she unlocked the door.

He pushed the door open and reached in to find a switch. "Let me look around before you go in."

Mariel followed while he checked each room, making

sure all the windows and doors were locked.

"Nice place."

"Thank you."

"Will you be all right alone? Should I call anyone?"

"It must be after midnight. I'll sleep with my cell phone under my pillow."

"You do that. Here's my card. I'll write my phone number on the back." He reached into his pocket for a pen. When he handed the card to her, his fingers brushed hers. "Give me a call when you're ready to go in tomorrow."

She looked at the card.

"Lock your door."

"I will."

She closed the door and leaned against it, taking several deep breaths. Zack Leoni. Her unlikely hero. What were the chances of that?

She was eighteen when she saw him last.

After years of hero-worship, she'd been devastated by his rejection. She'd been so sure of a positive response.

He'd been so hot, and she'd been so ready to take the next step with him.

A quiet rejection would have hurt. The very public rejection made it ten times worse.

She still hadn't forgiven him. She hadn't even forgiven herself for making such a stupid move.

But he'd been there for her tonight.

She went to bed, leaving all the lights on.

Chapter 3

*Trust yourself, you know more than you
think you do.
--Benjamin Spock*

Mariel opened one eye, then the other. Sunlight flooded the room, warming the corners where shadows normally lurked. The clock on her bedside table read ten o'clock. She threw back the covers and jumped out of bed. She'd missed church after promising her mother she would be there.

So how did you think you'd get to church in Napa—walk the twenty miles?

She plopped back into bed and snuggled under the warm covers. The phone would jar her awake in a half hour if she happened to fall back to sleep. It would be her grandmother, scolding her for missing church and for being a trial to her mother. Nana Reynoso, who claimed to have "the sight," would tell her she saw hens walking in a row across the street, ignoring a worm on the sidewalk. She would assign dire meaning about lost opportunities.

Mariel was positive Nana made up most of her stories.

What would her grandmother say about last night? That she predicted it? That no good can come of being out at all hours and driving home alone? *Amen to that.*

She closed her eyes, and tried to relax so she could remember the sequence of events, so she wouldn't forget an important clue. Had she offended anyone at the party? Had she ticked off any coworkers during the week? What about Lane? Would he stoop so low as to try to scare her on a lonely road at night?

No. It had to be random...the stranger Zack had mentioned.

She tossed the covers aside and dangled a leg over the edge of the bed. The other leg followed, and she put both feet on the cool floor and pushed herself up. The bulky sweatshirt she'd slept in had served as armor in her mind. Now she was almost too hot while she padded around the condo in her bare feet, turning off lights as she went.

Her phone rang. Nana? She looked at the number. Nope, it was Mama.

"Mariel, I expected to see you in church this

morning." Her mother's voice projected a hint of disapproval.

"I'm sorry, Mama." She decided not to mention her scare yet.

"Will you be over for dinner? We're eating early. Your papa has to get up early to go to Mendocino tomorrow."

"I'll try, Mama. I have a few things to do today."

"On Sunday? You're not going in to work, are you? How was the party last night?"

"It was great, Mama. The party went well."

"You don't sound very enthusiastic."

"I'm only tired. I got home late."

"I'll set a plate for you. Call if you decide not to come."

Mariel put down the phone and headed for the kitchen. Sunday dinners were a tradition. Even her sisters tried not to miss them when they were home.

She checked her purse for Zack's card.

Zachary Leoni, Deputy Sheriff.

His eyes still sparkled with mischief, and his mouth seemed fixed in a secret smile. He'd always made her heart do flip-flops, even when he was a tall, skinny teenager, always eating and making little jokes. Then he went out for football, and his body developed into something created by a master sculptor. She remembered when he and Sam had contests to see who could do the most push-ups.

He'd become one hot property.

Don't kid yourself. He still is.

She sat at her counter and sipped her coffee, nibbling on a piece of toast. Last night's incident still made her shudder. Reynoso women were strong. She would not let one bad experience take over her life.

Getting up, she plugged her smartphone into a speaker and found an old recording by the Romero brothers. The soothing sounds of Spanish guitars filled her with the need to move and she began to sway to the seductive sounds, her legs moving freely from the bottom of the long sweatshirt.

Dancing was her salvation. Whenever she was sad or moody, she let music fill her senses and call out to her body through bold rhythms. And when she was through, she could go about her daily routine with a relaxed smile.

It worked its magic again.

In the shower she let hot water pound into her back and shoulders, finishing the release of tension begun by her dance. She reached for her shampoo and worked it into her long hair. After rinsing, she stepped out, toweled, and slipped into a soft terry cloth robe. It was time to call Zack.

Pulling a short-sleeved cotton sweater over her head, she shimmied into jeans and dried and brushed her hair to a bright luster. This was not a date, she reminded herself. She didn't care what Zack thought of her. After today she would be sure to stay far, far away from him.

She reached for the phone and punched in the number. He answered right away.

"Leoni."

"It's Mariel."

"How did you sleep?"

"I slept okay. I'm ready to talk to other people."

"I'll be there in forty-five minutes."

* * *

The gray sedan pulled up right on time. Mariel grabbed her purse and went out to meet him, locking the door carefully behind her.

Zack got out of his car and stood waiting for her, ever the gentleman as he opened the door on the passenger side.

"You look a lot better today," he said after she got in the car.

"I should think so. I didn't have anyone try to kill me this morning."

He paused before closing the door.

"The creep wasn't trying to kill you, Mariel. He was trying to get you to stop so he could assault you. Have you taken any classes in self-defense?"

"Why would I? I don't have enemies. I'm twenty-three years old. I haven't lived long enough to offend anyone."

"Knowing you, I'd say that's probably true. I, on the other hand, am only four years older than you are, and I've offended plenty of people. But you should consider the training."

He didn't smile when he said it. She had trouble imagining who he could have offended. Certainly not a woman. All he had to do was grin and any woman would grovel at his feet.

She sat back and allowed the hum of the engine to lull her into an uneasy peace.

* * *

They drove in silence. Zack glanced at Mariel and shifted in his seat when he thought about all that hair spread on a pillow. He remembered how it felt tucked against his neck, and her particular scent when he carried her into his house. Mariel looked out the passenger window, her hands pressed tightly together in her lap.

"Not nervous, are you? The sergeant on duty is going to be very straightforward. He'll ask you for the facts. Nothing more. You can do that, can't you?"

"I guess so." She took a deep breath and worried her lower lip with her teeth. His hand tightened on the steering wheel.

"I'll be right there with you. He'll ask me questions, too."

Zack parked in the visitors' space, got out, and came around to open her door.

The substation was new, right off the main highway. He hadn't been in the building for a month. *Administrative leave pending the completion of an independent investigation.* Nice term for screwing up. He only hoped the conclusion would clear him so he could get on with his life.

Right now he was treading water, not sure if he should even be a cop. Most of his colleagues knew who they were and what they wanted. He was still struggling. What seemed like the right career before his reserve unit was called up no longer held the same appeal.

Depending on what the investigators concluded, he might not have a choice.

Zack buzzed himself in, with Mariel following. Three deputies in uniform sat at desks with stacks of paper next to small laptop computers. One stood up when they came in.

"I thought you were on leave, Leoni." He turned to Mariel, holding out his hand. "Sgt. James Carlyle. Have a seat." He gestured toward a chair opposite his desk. Zack grabbed a chair from a corner of the room and sat next to her.

"Leoni called this in last night, but he didn't have details. I need you to tell me in your own words exactly what happened."

Mariel told her story, apologizing several times for not remembering everything. Her voice quavered. Zack watched her and nodded from time to time, trying to reassure her, knowing she probably didn't want any help from him.

"Do you have any reason to believe someone you know wants to harm you?"

"No. No one."

"Without a good description of the perpetrator or a license plate number, there's not much to go on. You understand that, don't you Ms. Reynoso?"

"Yes."

The deputy turned off his recorder and stood up. "I'm sure Leoni told you, this is not the first report we've had from women on isolated roads late at night. But this looks like an escalation. If you think of anything else that might be helpful, please give me a call." He handed her a card. "And be careful."

"Thank you." She shook his hand again, then followed Zack toward the lobby.

A voice called out from across the room. "Hey, Leoni. Been to any boxing matches lately?" Laughter followed.

He stiffened and didn't respond. Eyes forward, he grabbed Mariel's arm and guided her through the door.

* * *

Mariel glanced at Zack and noted his clenched jaw.

Why would a simple comment make him tense? By the time they reached the car, he seemed to relax.

"Now that wasn't too bad, was it?" he said.

"No, but I still feel vulnerable."

"You were a convenient target. That's all." He put his arm around her and gave her a quick squeeze. She stiffened. "I'll bet nothing like this will ever happen again, but promise me you'll take the long way home from now on. The road through Napa is much safer."

"You bet I will."

They drove in silence all the way back to Zack's. He drove into his garage so she could turn her car around easily in the driveway.

"Would you like to come in for a minute?"

Was he serious?

Mariel held out her hand and used her professional tone of voice. "Thank you, Zack. I don't know what I would have done without you." He grasped it and looked down into her eyes until her breath caught.

"If I say, 'just doin' my job, ma'am,' I'll sound like a TV cop. So I'll stick to 'you're welcome' and leave it at that."

He brushed her cheek with his fingertips. Warmth stole through her. She had a sudden urge to wrap her arms around him and feel the hard planes of his body against her own. What was wrong with her? This man had humiliated her in the worst way.

He hesitated. "I know we haven't talked about...you know...but I want you to know I'm really sorry."

She looked at her feet, her cheeks starting to flame.

"I shipped out with my unit the next day, leaving you stuck here to face everyone alone." He paused. "I owe you. If there's ever anything I can do to make up for that please tell me."

She looked up and saw his mouth curve into a warm smile, but quickly looked away. She didn't want to talk about that night. Not ever.

Mariel started her car and slowly backed out of his driveway. She could see him in her rear view mirror, watching until she turned onto the road leading down the hill, back toward Sonoma. In broad daylight it didn't seem as scary as last night.

Was it only last night? How could something so traumatic fade so quickly? Maybe it was the replacement of terror with irritation. Zack still stirred something in her. She wasn't sure what it was, but it was there, ready to bloom with a little nurturing. She absolutely could not let that happen. But he'd been gracious and owned up to the fact that she'd been stuck with facing the humiliation alone.

Damn right he owed her.

Instead of going back home, Mariel drove to her office. La Golondrina Winery was located in the Carneros region, near the county line between Napa and Sonoma. She'd run in and pick up the flat-heeled shoes she left there before the party, then be on her way.

Sunday was a busy day in wine country. The parking lot was full, plus a minibus with tourists from San Francisco was parked at the side.

The tasting room was new, although the barrel room full of fermenting wine had carved casks as old as the wine industry. A two-story stone building was all that was left of the original winery site. The new part had a sleek, modern tasting room with a stainless steel serving bar making a full circle in the center of the room. Outside, fountains danced next to a flat terrace dotted with umbrella-shaded tables. A few people picnicked outside, while others sampled wine inside at the circular bar.

"Hey, you want to crawl in here and give us a hand?" The question came from a pretty girl with short blond hair who was serving a group of young men.

"Looks like you've got everything under control. I'm technically not here."

"Okay, Mariel. Wait 'till you need my expert advice on a wine pairing."

Mariel laughed and breezed on through, noting that Jessica, her best friend, was having a grand time with her customers.

She dodged a couple of women coming out of the rest room and made it to the end of the hall to a door marked Offices. Hers was toward the back, but she didn't mind. She had a great view of the vineyards, when she could see them. Today boxes of glassware were stacked in front of the window and different napkin samples were strewn on a tabletop. She hadn't had time to put things in order before the party started last night.

Her door burst open and Jess waltzed in, perching on the corner of her desk.

"Guess who came in today looking for you?"

It could only be one person. "I thought Lane was in L.A."

"Nope. He's here. I reminded him you didn't work Sundays." Jess adjusted her skirt with a sly smirk. "So who's that gorgeous guy I saw you driving with this afternoon?"

"When did you see that?" Jess was as bad as Nana.

"I came in at one o'clock, and I was right behind you for a few miles. Cars don't move very fast on Sundays around here, so I had plenty of time to get a good look."

"His name is Zack Leoni, and he's a deputy sheriff from Sonoma County." She had only met Jess two years ago. She didn't know about her grand humiliation.

"Where did you meet a cop?"

"Last night after the party."

"Wow, you move fast. You barely finished dumping Lane, and now you're with the cop?"

"I broke up with Lane two months ago." And she certainly wasn't with that particular cop. She told Jess what had happened, accepted a quick hug before she went back to the tasting room, and cautioned her to be careful when she was out at night.

Lane's early arrival was another problem.

She stared at a spot on the wall while an idea stirred in her brain.

She needed a fake boyfriend...one who was big and intimidating and believable. Zack said he owed her. Did she dare ask him to play the part? It would only be for the short time Lane was in town.

The old gossip would be front and center if they ran into anyone who remembered. They'd have to concoct some plausible story about how and why they were together.

It would be dicey, but it might work.

If he'll do it.

She picked up her phone and called Zack before she lost her nerve. It went to message.

"Hi, it's Mariel. Are you by chance available for lunch tomorrow? I want to thank you for saving me from that creep. My treat. Meet me at noon at La Golondrina, or text me if you can't make it."

This was as nerve-wracking as the tailgater. The last person she wanted to hang out with was Zack Leoni, but her need was greater than her discomfort would be.

If she could truly convince Lane she was in a relationship, maybe he'd leave her in peace. His crew was on location here for only a few more weeks. With luck, he'd be gone soon after.

Or maybe this was simply another of her ill-thought-out, impulsive ideas.

She swallowed and headed out the door.

Mama's pot roast was waiting.

Chapter 4

The strength of a family, like the strength of an army, is in its loyalty to each other.
--Mario Puzo

Mariel parked in front of her family's ranch style house in an older neighborhood of Napa. She turned off the ignition and sat for a moment under the cool canopy of her favorite leafy apple tree. A sense of security cloaked her while she crossed the sidewalk where she played hopscotch as a child and headed for the row of welcoming wicker chairs on the front porch. Nothing said home more than this neighborhood of deep lots with room for vegetable gardens beyond their back lawns.

The nervous tick in her left eye reminded her today was different. She would relive last night's experience once again and Mama would urge her to move back home.

She would resist.

She took a deep breath and knocked twice before opening the door. The aroma of cooked beef laced with exotic spices and the sounds of soft jazz coming from a CD player soothed her senses. Leave it to Mama to make the world right again.

"Hey, anyone home?"

"We're out back."

Mariel followed her mother's voice to the kitchen door. Outside, Papa and her eight-year-old nephew Nicky sat at the redwood picnic table, hunched over a game board. With school out, he was visiting for a week while his parents took a long-delayed honeymoon in Hawaii.

Mama looked up and waved while she watered her herb garden with a bright yellow can. Mariel rolled her shoulders to ease her tension and walked out to visit the group.

"Sit down. Take a load off." Her father didn't look up, but stayed focused on the game, his hand poised above the board while he decided his next move.

"Aunt Mariel, you missed church." Nicky's sunny grin told her he forgave her for not being there.

"I know I did. Sorry."

"The singing was great, wasn't it Grandpa?"

Papa responded with a grunt of assent, which must have pleased Nicky, because Papa was still staring at the board as though willing the checkers to move without touching them.

"Checkers? Not a video game?"

Nicky shrugged. "Grandpa doesn't like video games."

"I see."

She sat next to her father and patted his shoulder while she observed the game. He might be a legend in Napa Valley viticulture, but he was simply Papa to her. She studied his sun-browned face with wrinkles creasing his forehead and his bushy gray eyebrows knotted in concentration. Today he looked tired. His shoulders drooped and silver stubble glinted on his chin in the sunlight.

He worked too hard. He had no sons to help run his vineyard management company, and he'd always said it would not be one of his daughters. Paige could have run his business if she hadn't married. She knew viticulture as well as he did, and lately he'd allowed her to help...a good sign.

A yelp of glee pierced her reverie.

"I won. I won." Nicky jumped up hopped around the table.

"Fair and square, *niño*."

"What's all the commotion about?" Mama took off her cotton gloves and set them on the table.

"I beat Grandpa."

"This must be your day. First, you sing beautifully in church, and now you win your board game. What next?"

"Can I call Dad and tell him?"

"I guess so. You might tell your mother, too. She likes to hear about your day. When you're through, Grandpa can take you to Ryan's house. His father said to deliver you about five o'clock."

"Going to Ryan's for a sleepover?" Mariel asked.

"Yup. And pizza."

"Don't eat too much."

Nicky snorted and headed for the phone.

Mariel got up from the table and followed her mother into the kitchen. The subtle scent of chocolate and ginger in her mother's favorite cake could be detected beneath the more prevalent smells of the main course. Mama filled a bowl with hot potatoes, ready for mashing. Mariel felt a rumble deep in her stomach.

"When are Lindsay and Chris coming back?" She opened a drawer, pulled out a half apron and tied it around her waist.

"Next Saturday, but it won't be soon enough for Nicky." Mama wiped her hands on a towel and handed her a whisk. "You can stir the gravy," she said. "I'll finish the potatoes so I can face you while we talk."

Mariel teased. "I thought you could see with your back turned. Didn't you always tell us you had a second pair of eyes in the back of your head, so we'd behave ourselves?"

"That was when you and your sisters were younger and needed four eyes on you to keep you out of trouble."

"Mama, you astound me. I, for one, was an angel."

"An angel who occasionally sprouted horns and a tail."

Mariel laughed. "But you and Papa were always there to get me back on track, weren't you? And see?" She twirled. "No horns or tail now."

How safe and secure she had always felt in this kitchen. Some of her best memories were with her sisters, Lindsay and Paige, mixing cookie dough, throwing chocolate chips at one another, and arguing over which cleanup jobs each would do.

She missed her sisters now that they were married.

"Speaking of trouble, what's going on? You sounded a little tense when I called you this morning."

Mariel hesitated. She didn't want to repeat her story again for her father. Best to wait until they were all seated at the dinner table. Thinking about last night's chase caused goose bumps. Would the reaction ever wear off?

Her mother paused. "You shuddered, Mariel. This must be serious. Pour that gravy into a bowl and take it into the dining room. I'll be right in, and we'll talk."

On Sundays, her mother always brought out the good china and silver serving pieces. The ritual was something to rely on, like golden poppies opening in the sun. For Mariel the tradition was a constant in her harried life that was somehow comforting.

She lifted the heavy bowl of gravy and set it on a trivet in front of her father, who'd just come into the room was now seated in his usual chair.

Mama came in with a steaming platter of sliced meat surrounded by carrots and green beans. Dipping back into the kitchen, she returned with the potatoes. A bottle of wine was open, and Mariel poured herself a generous glass.

After saying grace, the food was passed around, and Mariel filled her plate. She had eaten only a piece of toast this morning and was starving.

"Out with it. What's going on that has upset you?"

Mama's intent stare made her feel like a bug under a microscope. Papa sipped his wine and said nothing while he waited for her to answer her mother's question.

"I had a bad experience with a guy last night." She was aware that she clutched her glass a little too tightly, so she relaxed her hold. The stem was fragile.

"What kind of experience?" asked her father.

"The guy nearly ran me off the road."

She told her story, keeping it brief. Both parents

stilled, neither able to speak. Mama's hand was over her mouth and Papa grasped his knife like he wanted to stab something.

"I turned into the Leoni's driveway and honked the horn. They're the only people I knew on Trinity Road, and I was very lucky someone was home."

Mama frowned. "You should have called me right away. I would have come over."

"It was not a comfortable night, but I got through it, and I'm much better today."

Papa looked perplexed. "I heard the Leonis moved to Oregon. Is that not true?"

"You heard right." Heat stained her cheeks. "The only one left there is Zack."

Mama twisted her napkin. "But he's the one…"

"Yes, Mama, he is." She wanted to stare back, but looked away. Her parents were in the audience that night, and had been mortified by what they heard. Her ears still rang from the scolding.

"You're not taking up with him again, are you?"

"I never 'took up with him,' as you so politely put it." This was still embarrassing, and would be even more so if he consented to help her with her plan.

Papa fixed both of them with his stare. "He was home when you needed him. That's all I care about. And let that be the end of the subject." He picked up his fork.

"Do you want to move back home?" Mama's tone was

gentle.

Mariel knew this offer was coming. It would be so easy to let her parents make decisions for her, but she had to fight it. They had always been protective, but she couldn't imagine moving back in with them now. Her independence was very important to her, and she needed to prove she could take care of herself.

But it was tempting.

Her sister, Lindsay, had moved out only recently, but she had a good reason for living at home. She had a child who needed a stable home while her job took her away for weeks at a time. That was before she and Nicky's father found each other again.

"No, Mama, I'm fine. The police said I was merely a random target."

"If you say so, but know the invitation is open."

Was she really all right? Residual fear still crouched beneath the surface and seemed to surface at the least provocation.

Tamp it down.

Her thoughts wandered to Zack, and the tingling of her nerve endings reminded her of the message she'd left. Would there be a resounding "no" among her messages? She hoped not. She needed this charade to convince Lane he was wasting his time pursuing her. If she seemed to be committed to someone else, it wouldn't seem like she was rejecting him.

And that was important. In fact, it was critical.

La Golondrina Winery was owned by a syndicate. The primary owner and managing partner was a television producer whose memorabilia covered the walls and drew guests to the tasting room. But there were three actors as well who were part owners. Lane was one of them. If he was feeling vindictive, he had enough power to keep her from getting her promotion. She didn't think he would do it, but she was feeling vulnerable right now.

She shut off her negative thoughts and helped her mother clean up before she left. After last night, she was drained, and wanted nothing more than to snuggle up with her pillow and close her eyes.

Rolling down her window to get a blast of cool air in her face, she merged into the traffic on Highway 29 and headed home, knowing tonight she was sure to sleep.

She had a full day tomorrow, and she needed all her energy.

Chapter 5

The winery was quiet when she arrived at work the next day, but it would be full by the time the first tour bus arrived at ten o'clock. She passed the tasting room with its crystal glasses gleaming on the circular bar and its blackboard with the day's tasting order written in chalk. First the white wines, then the reds. Tiny crackers were available to cleanse the palate between each taste.

The door to her office hid a desk littered with papers. In summer the winery hummed with wedding receptions, anniversary parties, and wine club dinners. Mariel juggled a schedule that depended on good weather and caterer availability. Most clients wanted their event to be outdoors amid the winery's fountains against the backdrop of leafy vineyards. If only there were more Saturdays in the summer months, then everyone would be happy.

She set down her purse and opened a poster-sized box propped in her chair to find reproductions of a half dozen paintings. An art show was scheduled for the event room in a month, and she hadn't even started working on the opening reception. Her biggest concern right now was the winery's annual party, which was held each year to raise funds for one of the local nonprofits. In a few days the owners would dine in the barrel room to decide on this year's recipient. Thank God that event was ready to go.

She cleared a space on her desk and prepared to make a list for the day. The pencil in her hand tapped against the pad. Was she nervous? Hell, yes. What if Zack doesn't show?

What if he does?

Most of her phone messages were about the annual party. The florist had ordered special hothouse flowers to fit the Hawaiian theme, but Plumeria might not be available. Could she choose something else just in case? The caterer would be roasting pork in the ground. Was there a backhoe available to dig the pit? Did they want etched glasses for the guests to take home, or should they use generic wine glasses?

She'd call them back this afternoon.

Immersing herself in her routine helped her get through the morning, although she wished she could put on her headphones and a leotard and dance her way out of the very bad feeling that had come over her. Was she being impulsive again? Was she on the verge of another bad decision?

"So this is where you hang out during the day." The deep tones flowed over her like molten honey, making her sigh in relief.

"Hey, thanks for coming."

"I don't turn down invitations that include food." When he grinned, an enticing dimple appeared. She felt his heat across the room.

Maybe this isn't such a good idea.

In her mind, she'd practiced what she'd say to convince him to help her. It would be temporary—two weeks at the most. They wouldn't have to spend much time together, except to establish the relationship in the minds of others. In public they'd have to appear at least affectionate. And when Lane saw she was committed, he'd look for someone else. Lane had an ego the size of Texas, but he wasn't a bad person. When he saw she'd moved on, she and Zack would never have to see each other again.

What she hadn't practiced was how to turn off her emotional reaction to him. Years ago, she'd thought herself in love with Zack and he'd hurt her. She had to make sure she didn't make the mistake of falling for him again.

He leaned against the wall at the back of the room as if surveying her space, arms folded, head slightly cocked, one foot crossed over the other. He looked like a man who was comfortable in his own skin and didn't much care what others thought.

Right now he looks downright sexy.

He caught her staring and his eyes seem to soften, holding her gaze. She looked down, willing herself to remember how often she'd told herself she disliked him.

Willing herself to believe it.

Failing.

The door next to Zack burst open, and the man she'd hoped not to see for at least a few more days sauntered in, his cocky smile as fake as his fake snakeskin boots.

Lane Brody strolled up to her desk and reached out as if to touch her. "Hey there, twinkle toes. You're not hiding from me, are you?"

Mariel scrambled to her feet and backed away, her eyes darting toward Zack, who'd straightened up, his expression concerned. Lane hadn't noticed him.

"I didn't expect to see you until Wednesday," she said while she inched her way around the edge of her desk and moved slowly toward Zack. Getting her cue, he lifted himself from the wall and cleared his throat.

He extended his hand while he walked up to Lane. "I

don't believe we've met."

Lane looked at Mariel while he automatically shook Zack's hand, then dropped it.

"Who's this guy?"

She swallowed and said a silent prayer that Zack would go along with her. She put her arm around his waist and leaned into him, looking back at Lane. "Lane Brody, this is Zack Leoni."

Lane halted, a smirk on his face. "What's he...your bodyguard?"

"I guess in a way he is. He's a Sonoma County Deputy Sheriff. He's also my boyfriend."

The stricken look came and went in an instant. He laughed and picked up her left hand. "Yeah? Well at least I don't see a ring on that finger yet."

Zack's arm stiffened on her shoulders, but he said nothing. Mariel was afraid to glance at his expression, afraid of what she'd see.

"We were on our way out to grab some lunch before doing a little house-hunting," she said.

She prayed that Zack wouldn't let her down. She needed to convince Lane she was in a serious relationship.

Lane's eyes narrowed as he looked at Zack.

"That's right. And we're going to be late if we don't leave right now, aren't we honey." He dropped his arm, grabbed Mariel's hand and tugged.

She raised her eyebrows at an astonished Lane, plucked her purse off her desk, and headed out the door. "You can find your way out, can't you, Lane?"

"Nice meeting you, Mr. Brody," Zack said as Mariel pulled him down the hall and out into the parking lot.

Mariel dropped his hand and stopped to take a few deep breaths. She glanced up at his smile. "I can explain."

"I can hardly wait."

* * *

Murphy's Irish Pub off the Plaza in Sonoma was clearing out. They sat down at an outdoor table next to a pedestrian walkway away from street noise.

He watched Mariel fiddle with her purse and roll her napkin into a little ball, all the while looking away. The ride over had been silent.

He had lots of questions.

What the hell is she up to?

She picked up the menu and lifted her head to look directly into his eyes. He was struck again by how beautiful she was…her eyes as green as a summer meadow and her lashes as dark as midnight. Today her hair was pulled back from her face and held by a red ribbon. Her sisters were pretty, but Mariel had the face and body of a film star. He could easily see her with a guy like Lane Brody.

Not with a guy like me.

He dismissed that thought. She'd been out of his league, even when they were still friends, and now, with his career hanging by the proverbial thread, he had even less to offer any woman, let alone one like Mariel. Besides, he knew she hadn't quite forgiven him for what happened in the past…not yet.

"Are you ready to tell me what's going on? What's this boyfriend thing all about?"

She put both her hands on the table and leaned closer. "On Sunday you said you owed me, that all I had to do was ask if I needed your help."

"True."

Where was this going?

"I need your help." She paused as if trying to find the right words. "I need you to pretend to be my boyfriend…for only a couple of weeks."

"You practically told that guy we were moving in together."

"I know. I thought it would make him think we're serious." She took a deep breath. "I can play a part, can you?"

Could he?

His thoughts wandered back to the infamous talent show. Mariel had always been the kind of girl who made people feel good—always busy, always talking, always happy. Seeing her all grown up for the first time, he'd become an instant admirer, especially when she turned that charm on him.

Playfulness had escalated into flirtation. And in a stolen moment at the party the night of the dress rehearsal, he'd kissed her. He hated himself the moment he did it, because he'd promised her cousin he would watch out for her. She had a reputation for getting herself into trouble back then. Apparently, she hadn't grown out of that tendency.

He shook his head. Could he do this? Spending time with her wasn't a problem. Right now he had nothing but time. Touching her, kissing her, breathing the air she breathed. That would be a problem.

"Let's order, and then you tell me what this is all about."

"I don't have much of an appetite."

She had a nervous habit of biting that luscious lower lip with her perfect white teeth. Zack caught himself wondering what it would feel like to have those teeth nipping at his earlobe or maybe his neck.

Stop it.

He turned to the menu to check out the offerings. "You have to keep your strength up, as my mother always said."

"Your mother was sweet, but she wasn't around much. You were the one at home when I came over to hang out with Keira."

"My mother always worked. I had babysitting duty."

Mariel feigned an indignant look. "We weren't babies."

"Pests, more like it."

"And you loved every minute of the attention. Admit it."

Her fingers brushed his wrist as she spoke, sending little tendrils of heat along his arm. The animation in her face was contagious, making him want to smile into those beautiful eyes.

Zack swallowed. It had been a long time since his gut fluttered like a lovestruck teen. Ordinarily, he'd enjoy it. But the timing was wrong…and what the hell would he say to Sam? Oh, it's only a *temporary* arrangement. It's not *real*. It's only another one of Mariel's harebrained schemes. *Of course* I'll keep my hands off her.

He rechecked the menu. "I'll order my lunch, and then I'll order a salad for you. If you're not hungry, you can give it me. How does that sound?"

He loved her relaxed, open expression, and the way she tilted her head, as if eager to hear his next comment. She was being nice to him today because she needed him. Maybe if he helped her, she'd forgive him for leaving her to face everyone alone.

In your dreams, Leoni.

He gave their order and then gave into temptation and placed his hand over hers. She removed her hand and tucked it under her napkin.

"You're worried about this guy, so tell me the story."

Her good mood faded, and he cursed himself for getting right to the point. He had never been known for his tact, one of his problems with his job. He focused on Mariel's hair, the sun glinting on red highlights when she moved her head.

No harm in staring.

Mariel picked up her fork and tilted it in the sunlight. "I took a job as a pourer in the tasting room at La Golondrina while finishing my second year of college. It was fun, and I got to meet a lot of people and it got me out of my parents' house. I started working there full time and last year I was put in charge of the winery's events. That's when I met Lane Brody. He's one of the owners."

Zack watched her play with the fork, running her finger along its edge. Her expression was troubled. A frown line marred her forehead.

"When Lane began to pursue me, I was flattered. We hooked up." She swallowed. "I soon realized I'd made a mistake and broke it off. My values are not the same as Lane's crowd. I didn't understand it at the time. I do now."

She put down the fork and picked up the knife, rubbing its surface with gentle strokes. His breath caught as he imagined those fingers on... "Let me guess. He didn't like the fact that you walked away and he wants you back."

She looked up at him, her beautiful green eyes wide. "Lane can be very manipulative, and he makes up the rules as he goes along. I thought if I could convince him I was in a committed relationship, he'd give up."

An uncomfortable thought entered his head. "Maybe the guy's in love with you."

Mariel snorted. "The only person Lane loves is himself. My defection hurt his image as a hottie. I'm sure his ego told him he needed to be the one who ended the relationship."

"You're not afraid of him, are you?"

She looked up. The crease between her brows deepened. "Lane's persistent, but he's not violent, although he does like to play games."

He was getting a bad vibe from her. The cop in him imagined all kinds of scenarios, and none of them were good.

Sam's words from years past rang in his ears. *She's the fragile one, the one who trusts people to do the right thing. When they don't, she gets hurt.*

"You might want to consider that self-defense training I suggested. It looked like Lane was going to try to put a move on you today. A session or two might help you get away if he gets a little overeager."

She moved her spinach around with her fork. "Where do I get that kind of training?"

"I could teach you." *Now why did I offer to do that?* "Give it some thought. Let me know."

He switched the conversation to neutral subjects… Keira, his parents, improvements he was making in the house. When she started asking questions about his job, he changed the subject.

He had a disciplinary hearing in a couple of weeks for using his fist. He wasn't proud of what he'd done, but strict rules had always been a problem. In this job, he had to follow procedure. Because he hadn't finished his probation when he left, he was put back on probation when he returned.

There would be consequences.

He focused on Mariel, who preceded him out of the restaurant. He liked watching her walk, slightly on her toes, as if she were about to lift her arms and pirouette. Her skirt clung slightly to her bottom, and her long-sleeved blouse billowed in the breeze. His breath caught as he remembered the feel of her body against his chest when he carried her into the house.

This charade isn't going to be easy.

They rode back to the winery and went in through a busy tasting room. Zack was aware of the hard stare of a little blonde working behind the counter. Mariel waved at her and kept walking. When they got inside her office, she closed the door again, and turned toward him.

"What's your answer?   Will you help me? Can you and I pull this off?"

She made him smile with her eager expression. He couldn't help himself. Without touching her with his hands, he leaned down and kissed her cheek. She stepped away.

"What are you doing?"

He winked. "Practicing."

"Then you'll do it?"

He grinned. "I will. And then we're square."

She wrapped her arms around him, pressing her body to his. Arousal curled in his groin before she stepped back.

"What are you doing?"

"Making sure you don't cringe and push me away if I do that."

He laughed. "Now, who in their right mind would step away from you?"

"I can think of someone," she said with a hint of sarcasm.

Heat crawled up his cheeks.

I deserved that.

Mariel liked to hug. Even as a kid, she'd been spontaneous. He remembered helping her with a math problem once, leaning over her shoulder while her pencil moved on the paper. When she grasped the concept, she'd jumped up and clung to him as if he'd saved her life.

He was shy then, a little overwhelmed by her.

Now he was a man who could have his career come crashing down on him in a couple of weeks, and he was going to play boyfriend with her? What was he thinking?

He said a quick goodbye, turned around and let himself out, stopping briefly at the men's room to splash water on his face and calm his raging hormones.

It didn't work.

Chapter 6

*A friend is someone who walks into a
room when everyone else is walking out.*
--Gary Moore

Zack dragged a dry log up a slope to his back yard. His
parents had let the trees and brush at the back of the
house get too thick. Fire season was upon them, and he
needed to clear a space around the house.

It also opened the view to the vineyards behind the
property.

He sat on a stump and surveyed the green vines
planted in neat rows in the field beyond. He
remembered when these grapes were planted. He'd been
five or six years old, trailing after the workers while they
installed the trellising, then planted each vine. The
young vines had seemed like sticks to him. Now they
were leafy and in full production.

After junior college, he'd considered going to a university with a good viticulture program, but a football scholarship from a school in another state couldn't be turned down, so he'd taken classes in police science. When he graduated he went to the Sheriff's Academy to become a deputy and started his probationary period. Then the Army Reserve unit he'd joined was called up, and his career in law enforcement was put on hold. At least when his tour of duty ended, he had a job to go back to. He was lucky. Some guys didn't.

Insisting on renting the house from his parents had been a good idea. Even with insurance, their bills were significant. Making steady payments over a long period of time would help them, even if it locked him into a job he wasn't sure he wanted.

One I might not even have by the end of the month.

His cell phone rang and he dug it out of his jeans pocket. He recognized the number. It was the police association's labor attorney.

"Leoni."

"Your hearing is only a couple of weeks away. We need to prepare. Can you come in this afternoon around three?"

"That would work. Should I bring anything?"

"Just yourself."

He put away the phone and picked up the ax.

Swinging hard, he split the log and stacked the wood in a wheelbarrow. He wouldn't use much in the summer, although some nights were cool. The house was old, and the heating system needed all the help it could get until he saved enough to get a new furnace.

And physical labor took his mind off his upcoming hearing.

He knew he'd have trouble transitioning back into normal life when he returned from combat in the mountains of Afghanistan, but it had been harder than he expected. He'd seen enough violence to last a lifetime.

Protect and serve.

Law enforcement required quick thinking and a calm response, with a dose of compassion thrown in. It had no room for hesitation, self-doubt, or inappropriate behavior, even if it was righteous.

Like decking a guy who'd beat up his kid and was working on his wife.

He couldn't believe he'd knocked the guy out. But he couldn't stand to see innocents hurt. He'd lost it, forgetting everything he'd been trained to do.

He could still hear his training officer's voice.

You're supposed to pull him off, not get between them. You're supposed to use your baton to subdue him, not your fists. You're supposed to call for backup if you can't handle it. What were you thinking? You're in deep shit, Leoni.

He pulled the shirt over his head and let the sun warm his back. He'd stack the wood later. Swiping his forehead with the back of his hand, he picked up his shirt and headed into the house.

He grabbed a bottle of water out of the fridge and walked into the living room. Sinking into his couch, he took a deep swig and leaned his head back on the cushions. The faint scent of coconut teased his nostrils. He turned and breathed deeply. It was her scent.

He closed his eyes and pictured Mariel lying on his couch. All his protective instincts had come out in full force the night she showed up in his driveway…along with a few baser ones. He shifted his position. Older memories of Mariel were safer.

She'd been a mischief-maker with a bouncy ponytail and endless energy when he first met her. She and his sister Keira had been constant companions—from middle school through high school—and always seemed to be hanging around him. In high school he'd considered her as pesky as his little sister. But when he entered the local community college, he started paying closer attention. She'd become a real beauty by then. Unfortunately, she was a good four years younger, as well as being his best friend's cousin. She'd been completely off limits.

And still is.

Sam Reynoso was like a brother. They'd both been

receivers on the high school and junior college football teams, always trying to outplay each other. Since he returned to the wine country, they'd shot pool, had a few beers, and taken a couple of short motorcycle trips up the coast. Sam was still very protective of his cousin Mariel. He said she needed someone to keep her out of trouble, and he'd promised his aunt he'd try.

Fake boyfriend? How was that going to sit with Sam? Zack would find out when he saw him tonight.

* * *

Law offices made Zack uncomfortable, especially ones in big cities. He was a country boy and the only other time he'd visited the office of a city lawyer was when his grandfather died and the family gathered for the reading of the will. The buildings looked the same to him...large, impersonal, sterile, and thoroughly intimidating.

He found the law firm on the sixth floor, its name on a stainless steel plaque on the wall next to the door. He was shown into a small room with a polished wooden table and two chairs. A pewter water pitcher with four glasses stood on a sideboard.

The door opened and a guy his own age came in, a sheaf of papers in his hand. "Zachary Leoni? I'm Jonah Brown."

They shook hands and the attorney sat down across from him. He set up a tablet with a keyboard and nodded at Zack congenially.

"As you know, our firm represents your union in all disciplinary matters. I've been assigned to guide you through the process."

He scanned the top document on a stack of papers. "You've received a verbal, and two written reprimands. Is that correct?"

"Yes."

"Why don't you tell me in your own words what happened on the night in question."

Zack closed his eyes and let images flow. "A 911 call came in from an address on Maple Drive in the hills north of Sonoma. I was dispatched. When I arrived I heard sounds of a fight. The door was open, so I went in."

His throat felt like a desert gulch. He swallowed and tried to be precise.

"I saw a juvenile lying on the floor. He was breathing, but unconscious. I called for an ambulance and a backup unit. Then I heard a scream, and I went to the rear of the house. The male suspect had a female pinned to the wall. Her eye was swelling and she was crying. I told him to stand aside. He ignored me."

"What happened then?" The attorney kept typing.

"The man bunched his fist and hit the woman in the stomach."

He didn't have a weapon, but Zack had approached

him carefully, his training kicking in. He remembered pulling him away and ordering him to sit in a chair. The guy had laughed and told him to get the fuck out of his house. Then he'd lunged toward the woman again.

Something had snapped. A flood of anger threatened to drown him. He couldn't breathe. Memory flashed. He was ten years old again stepping between his aunt and her scumbag husband, trying to protect her. Failing.

"Please answer Mr. Leoni."

"I pulled him off the female, but when he went for her again, I hit him in the face with my fist. He fell to the floor."

"Where was your training officer?"

"He'd been detained at a previous call. As we were in separate units, I was sent on ahead. It was a busy night."

The attorney paused. "You're aware that Mr. Callahan has filed a suit against the department for police brutality.

"I am. That's why I'm on leave pending the outcome of the investigation."

"And you're aware that Callahan claims you are the one responsible for his son's condition, that he tried to pull you away from his son, and that's when you hit him."

The pencil he was holding snapped in half. "No, I wasn't aware of that." His stomach clenched and bile rose in his throat. He stood and went to the window, looking out at the traffic below, willing himself to take deep breaths. How could he fight this? His backup hadn't arrived until after he knocked the guy on his butt.

"Deputy Leoni?"

Zack sat down and folded his hands under the table.

"The woman knows what really happened."

"You mean Mrs. Callahan?"

"I didn't get her name, but I figured it was the wife. Buckley took the report when he got there. I followed the ambulance to the hospital. They took the boy right to emergency. I didn't realize he was in a coma."

The attorney stopped typing. "Mrs. Callahan's story agrees with her husband's. She says her son, Michael, answered the door, smarted off, and you shoved him into the wall so hard he lost consciousness. She also said her husband didn't harm her."

"Yeah? Then how did she explain her black eye?"

"Walked into a door."

His jaw clenched and he spoke through his teeth. "She lying."

"You and I know what happened. The problem is we have to prove it." The attorney closed his tablet. "Is it true you recently returned from Afghanistan?"

"Six months ago."

"And the department cleared you to come back to work?"

"Yeah. They cleared me. What are you getting at?"

"You have a clean record. Callahan's attorney will try to make a case that you were not fit for duty. That you should have been sent to counseling. That the department was at fault for allowing you to return. Do you get my drift?"

Zack tensed and looked down. This was worse than he ever imagined.

"They are going to claim that you are a danger to society, that you have post-traumatic stress disorder. Now I'm going to ask you a question that you must answer honestly." He paused. "Do you?"

Zack looked deep into the eyes of the man sitting across from him.

"Absolutely not."

* * *

His career was toast.

When he got home, he showered, changed his clothes, and hopped on his Harley. The cool evening air calmed him while he took the turns on the narrow curvy road over the hills into Napa. He needed to unwind. He needed to talk to someone about his upcoming hearing. He also wanted Sam to know about his deal with Mariel.

Sam Reynoso lived outside Napa in the middle of a vineyard. The dirt road leading to his place, which was nestled near the river, was long and flat. Zack brought the bike to a stop, took off his helmet, propped it on the bike, and wandered around back. This time of evening, Sam liked to sit out on his back porch, drinking a glass of wine…usually his own.

"Got any more of that hooch you're drinking?"

"What brings you to these parts?" He got up, went into the house, and came back with another glass. Pouring from the unlabeled open bottle, he handed the glass to Zack.

"Thought I'd take a ride. I figured you'd be home on a Monday night."

"You figured right."

Zack pulled over a white plastic chair and sat. Raising the glass to his lips, he gave it the swirl, sniff, and sip test, holding the wine in his mouth for a few seconds before swallowing.

"Good. You make this?"

Sam's brows shot up. "What does that mean? If it's good it must be commercial?"

"I didn't say that."

"It's my 2014 zinfandel. Still a little young, but the grapes were from Haywood, so it should be fantastic in a year or two."

"Will you enter it in the Harvest Fair competition?"

"Next year. And it has to be entered in Sonoma. The grapes are from Sonoma Valley."

They sat in silence, enjoying the peace. Sam peered

over the rim of his glass. "Want to talk about it?"

"Talk about what?"

"Whatever's eating you. You didn't come over to talk about wine. So spit it out."

Zack stared into the red glow on the horizon, the last remnant of the setting sun. A mosquito buzzed around his ear. "Remember that incident I told you about…the one that gave me this leave with pay during the independent investigation?"

"Yeah. What about it?"

"The guy I nailed has lawyered up. Not only is he filing a suit charging police brutality against the department because I hit him. He also says I beat up his kid."

Sam pounded the arm of his chair. "That's bullshit. What does *your* lawyer say?"

"He says if it were only a matter of his word against mine, I probably wouldn't have a problem. But the wife is sticking by the husband."

"I can't believe this."

"I have the disciplinary hearing for punching the guy —which I admit—and now I have a serious criminal complaint against me."

"Will the brutality charge go to trial?"

"I doubt it. The guy's a well-connected member of the community. If his lawyer knows his client's penchant for violence, he'll settle out of court. But it depends on the kid." He paused. "He's in a coma. If he doesn't recover…"

Sam's hand gripped his shoulder. "He'll come around."

"God, I hope so. I still don't know what happened."

Even exonerated, he'd probably be asked to resign. And he would. He wouldn't embarrass the department, even if it meant disappointing his parents.

"No wonder you're down. I think you need a distraction. Nana Reynoso sent over some *chili con carne* and a batch of home-made *tortillas*."

Zack groaned. "Is her chili as hot as I remember?"

"She hasn't lost her touch, but I never ask her what she puts in it. She shakes her finger and tells me I don't want to know."

"You probably don't."

They went into the house, piled chili and tortillas into their bowls and sat at the old wooden kitchen table with mismatched chairs. They talked about Sam's homemade winemaking, the odds of the San Francisco Giants winning another World Series, and Sarah, Sam's friend since elementary school, who happened to make the best shortbread this side of Scotland.

Zack always felt at home with the Reynoso brothers. They treated him like family. Sam's parents lived in Calistoga now, and his brothers had moved away. Sam rented the cottage when he went to work for a well-known winery, and was earning a little extra by helping his uncle with his vineyard management business. He seemed happy.

"Hey, I hear you did a good deed."

"What was that?"

"I saw Uncle Pete this morning and he told me about Mariel's run in with the tailgater. She was pretty scared. Thanks for taking care of her." He sat back in the chair, a smirk on his face. "I wish I'd been there to see her face when she realized it was you."

Zack grinned. "It was touch and go."

"After all these years, she still hasn't forgiven you."

"That was loud and clear."

Sam's grin faded. "But you still did the right thing back then, even though the public part was a pure fluke. You were heading for a war zone the next day."

"I know. But she caught me off guard, and I blurted out the first thing that came into my head."

He still remembered the ill-fated words. *I'm just not into you, Mariel. Call me when you grow up.* Then he'd punctuated the rejection with nervous laughter, making it even worse.

Sam nodded. "That girl gets herself into more trouble. She needs brothers." He forked another bite of chili, managing to smile while he chewed. "I guess she's got two…me, and now you."

Zack looked away. If he got through his current mess,

he'd like to date Mariel. But his only real friend was sitting across from him, telling him to back off. Well not exactly, but being a big brother meant he'd have to tamp down the urge to pull her close and use his lips to chase away any bad memories she had.

His thoughts strayed back to the night he'd laid her down on his couch, the feel of her skin, and the scent of her hair. Her skirt had ridden up to her thighs, and her breasts had formed plump mounds over the edge of her bodice. Heat pooled in his groin.

"Hey…where did you go right now? Not back to your problems. You were smiling."

"Huh?" Sam's voice jerked him out of his daydream. He picked up a thin, flaky *tortilla* and filled it with chili, making a burrito. "I'm a bit tired." He bit into the fiery mixture and concentrated on eating. He could dream about Mariel later. Right now he needed something to put out the fire in his mouth.

"Got any beer?"

Sam laughed and brought two beers to the table. "The old gal still makes the best chili in Napa."

"If you say so. My taste buds are burned to a crisp. It will be awhile before I can taste anything."

"I'll tell her you said that. But then her voice will get low and she'll say, 'Zachary needed a jolt to bring him to his senses. His reaction to my chili is a sign.' "

"She still does that, huh?"

"All the time."

"Well maybe this time she's right."

"Yeah? What else is going on?"

"I had lunch with Mariel today."

Sam stopped chewing and raised his eyebrows. "No kidding. She *has* forgiven you, then."

Zack shook his head. "Not exactly. She has a problem and decided I was the one who could help her because I *owe* her."

Sam jabbed his fork in Zack's direction. "You don't owe her anything. She's the one who came on to you that night. What's going on with her now? It's not that creep who tailed her, is it?"

"No. Apparently the ex-boyfriend is back in town and giving her trouble, so she's manufactured a fake boyfriend to keep him at bay."

"Lane 'asshole' Brody. Another one of her brilliant decisions." Sam swallowed and cocked his head. "So who's the lucky dude?"

Zack rolled his eyes. "Me."

Chapter 7

Trust, but verify.
--Ronald Reagan

You've got marshmallows in your head instead of a brain if you think you're immune to Zack, yet here you are, ready to torture yourself.

Mariel stood outside the storage building her cousin used for his home wine-making. She'd taken off an hour early and changed, wondering how much skill went into self-defense training. Dancing kept her in good shape, but she wasn't strong. Zack said strength wasn't needed if you knew the tricks.

She'd already regretted the spontaneous hug she'd given him the day of their lunch, but his kiss on her cheek had startled her. Zack had a right to kiss her if they were in a pretend relationship. Her snarky comment after the hug would remind him he'd once rejected her.

What would a real kiss be like? Her nerves tingled and her toes curled thinking about it.

She'd checked her upcoming schedule. She'd be in the winery late several nights. Lane believed he was irresistible to women, so if he was still skeptical about her relationship with Zack, he might show up, hoping to dazzle her with his charm.

So she'd called Zack and told him she'd like the self-defense training if the offer was still open. She was sure she wouldn't need it to protect herself against Lane. But her run in with the tailgater still made her shaky.

Zack's motorcycle was parked by the door, a machine as powerful as the man who rode it. She swallowed and rubbed her palms against her shorts. Maybe this wasn't such a good idea.

Long-held resentment wasn't holding her back. She'd finally let it go. But Zack's sexuality drew her like a beacon on a dark night. If she wasn't careful, she'd end up where she was five years ago…rejected and hurting.

For her own peace of mind, she had to continue to keep herself emotionally aloof so when the fake relationship ended, her heart would be intact.

He'd be so easy to fall for.

She couldn't let that happen again.

She opened the door and surveyed the room. A stationery bicycle and a weight bench anchored one end. The other half had wine barrels and bottling equipment. The scent of wine filled the air.

Zack was doing push-ups on a thick mat in the center. She watched the play of his muscles, noting the power in his arms and back. He was so beautiful. It was hard not to stare at him, even though she'd been lecturing herself about remaining distant.

"Hey." She tossed her purse on an empty barrel and went all the way into the room. Zack looked up.

"Right on time."

Mariel watched him place a towel and two bottles of water on a weight bench. Grinning, he came toward her.

He was dressed in workout shorts and a thin T-shirt that clung to him like it was skin, outlining biceps and abs worthy of a wrestler. She wrenched her gaze from his body and focused on his serious face.

"Where's Sam?"

"He's at Sarah's. She's trying out a new recipe and needed an unbiased opinion."

"Unbiased opinion? Sam will eat anything she puts in front of him. I don't know how he keeps the weight off." Her gaze swept the room. "I didn't realize he'd made part of this room a gym. Maybe that's how he does it."

Zack draped his own towel over a chair and took up a position in the center of the room. "Are you ready?"

After a deep breath, she took baby steps forward until

she stood in front of him. "I guess so."

"We're going to concentrate only on self-defense. You don't have the strength to take anyone down."

"That's a relief."

He stood behind her, his breath caressing her ear while he wrapped his arms around her. She suppressed the impulse to lean back into him, but remained taut, waiting for instructions.

"If a guy wants to assault you, he'll often approach you from behind, and will grab you like this." He tightened his hold, pulling her against him. "He'll expect you to scream, but he won't expect you to fight back. So you'll have the element of surprise. Okay. Try to get away."

She wriggled in his grasp and tried to pry his hands loose, but he tightened them.

"What do I do?"

"Relax and go limp."

"Really?"

"Try it."

She did—feeling him stagger off balance. It gave her enough time to fall to the floor and turn.

"It feels awkward, but I guess it works."

"Not always. But it's better when it's not expected. I knew you were going to do it and subconsciously loosened my grip."

She stared up at him and grabbed his hand when he

offered it to pull her up. A few more tries and she felt comfortable with the move.

"What else can I do?"

He grinned. "You won't like this one. If you have a pencil or pen, or even a car key, you can use it to stab the eyes. In fact, if you're ever out alone in a vulnerable location, walk with one in your hand."

Horrified, she looked at him. "The eyes?"

"If someone has grabbed you, your purpose is to get away. Screaming. Yelling. Cursing. Anything to bring attention to you and get the help you need. A sharp jab to the eye will keep a guy distracted long enough for you to run."

He folded his fingers over her shoulders, positioning her body in front of him. "If someone grabs you from the front, there's a different technique."

His arms came around her, pulling her to his hard body. Every ridge and curve, even ones lower than his abs, teased her where they touched. Every point of contact sent frissons of heat right to her core. She wanted to rub herself against him, to see what his reaction would be.

Giving in to the impulse, she tightened her arms and flattened her breasts against his chest. He groaned and loosened his hold. Was he as affected as she was?

Of course not, he'd rejected her. This was business.

Then why does it feel so good?

He directed her to try to pull away.

"In this case, you bring your arms up fast underneath your assailant's and try to break his hold. Go ahead. Try it."

She brought her arms up, but was unable to escape.

"That didn't work. What else?" Her voice shook. She was sure her face was scarlet.

I shouldn't give in to my impulses.

"We'll practice until it feels right. Right now I want you to get your palm up and jab me in the nose. You probably aren't strong enough to break an assailant's nose, but it will hurt like hell."

"You really want me to try it?"

"Sure, but let's not put any force into it, okay? I'd hate to get blood all over Sam's nice clean mats."

His arms came around her, holding her against his body. She slid her hand up his thigh, inching it toward the center of his body, over a ridge that made her breath catch before she wiggled it up his chest and pushed it in his face.

"Gotcha."

He dropped his arms and stood back, turning away from her. She saw him breathing hard, like he was getting himself under control. "I can't believe a beautiful girl like you hasn't had a rape prevention class." His voice sounded hoarse.

"Guess I didn't think I needed one." She walked over

to the edge of the room, picked up one of the water bottles and drank. He rolled his shoulders and turned back around. "Ready for the next lesson?"

They went over a few more of the basic techniques taught in most classes—how to increase peripheral vision, how to find your best exit, how to increase awareness of your surroundings, and the use of basic items in her purse as weapons.

"If you have spray perfume, you can point it at the eyes. Sharp objects like keys or your nails…all can be used effectively. You can cup your hands and slap them over an assailant's ears and break their eardrums."

"I don't think I could do that."

He looked serious and softened his voice. "If you're in danger, you'd be surprised at what you can do. Think of your masked tailgater. What if he'd grabbed you?"

They practiced a few more moves, facing each other on the mat. Often their bodies touched. Mariel tingled in odd places, aware of his strength, and the gentle way he touched her, like a tentative lover who doesn't know how he'll be received.

When they were through, she grabbed the towel and waters from the bench while he pulled off his shirt and worked with Sam's weights.

What would it be like to have that gorgeous body all to herself? If she made a move would he reject her again? He had made it very plain that he still thought of her as Sam's little cousin.

But she was definitely no longer a little girl.

* * *

Zack finished his workout and sat up. Mariel was lying on her back with her eyes closed. Was she asleep? They'd worked out nearly two hours, refreshing basic techniques, their bodies meeting until his brain was scrambled and he could no longer focus.

Either that, or die of the pleasure.

When she entered the room she had on shorts that barely covered her butt and a tank top that clearly outlined her assets. When he first pulled her into his body from behind, her backside had nestled nicely against him and had wriggled as she tried to get free. The sensation had shot sparks through his hardening groin and he had to let her go or embarrass himself. Demonstrating frontal attacks had been worse, and he finally had to call a halt so he could turn away and think of ice and snow—anything that would make him decent again.

He finally gave up. She was tired and needed the rest, and a good workout with weights would keep his mind on track. When he finally sat up, there she was, lying on her back, and he might as well not have wasted his time on the weights, because all he could think about was lying down next to her, under her, on top of her.

It had to be their proximity. Too many hard pulls

against his body. Too many errant thoughts while trying to teach basic moves. But she was a quick learner, and he was sure she'd be reasonably safe.

But would he?

Her eyelids flickered. "Are you ready to call it a day?" he asked.

She sat up and finished her water. "I think I need a shower."

Geez, did she have to say that? Now all he would think about was how she would look naked, water running over that lush body, her hands full of soap suds.

"I could use one, too."

She gazed at him and sucked in her bottom lip. Turning, she picked up the towel and headed for the door.

"Do you want to continue tomorrow? Same time?"

"We can't. We have an event tomorrow."

"Nice of you to tell me, girlfriend." The mischief in his eyes took the sting out of his words. "What is it? Do I need a tux?"

She laughed, her eyes raking his body head to toe. "I'd love for you to come as you're dressed right now so Lane could see how wise it would be not to mess with you. But slacks and a collared shirt will do. It's a dinner in the winery's barrel room."

"Lane will be there?"

"Sure will, as will the other owners." She listed them

for him, watching his surprised expression.

"You certainly keep classy company."

"I'll be setting everything up, but I'm allowed to stay and bring a date for cocktails…so we'll have our first audience."

"What time shall I pick you up?"

"Around four if that's okay. I'm going home early to change. If we're back by five I can help set up."

"I'll practice my doting expression and make sure it never leaves my face."

"Me, too. We need to make good use of our time." Her lips curved into a seductive smile, and she twirled the towel while she walked away, her hips swaying.

Zack decided to do a few more push-ups before he went home.

Chapter 8

Trust is built with consistency.
--Lincoln Chaffee

The long concrete cave was lined with oak wine barrels stacked to the ceiling. The scent of the winery's signature merlot filled the air. Red velvet chairs faced each other on both sides of a long wooden table, and a web of white twinkle lights provided a soft glow overhead.

Zack and Mariel carried boxes of plates and glassware from her office to the dining area. Linens and silverware were next. The catering staff took over while Mariel put small baskets of flowers on the tables.

"You're a pretty useful guy to have around," she said. She took a cardboard box out of Zack's hands and opened it to carefully lift out an elaborate, blown-glass candleholder.

Zack watched her cradle the delicate piece, placing it carefully in the center of the table before putting white votive candles around it. "How did you get interested in event planning? I thought you wanted to be a professional dancer."

She slid the piece about two inches and stood back. "I did…once. Dreams don't always work out."

She stood back, her hands steepled. "It looks beautiful."

"Yes it does." He looked directly at her, not the table. For a moment their gazes met. Zack held his breath. Mariel was the first to look away.

Zack picked up a stack of empty boxes. "Where do you want these?"

"Back in my office. The caterer already unloaded and his crew will staff the bar and circulate with appetizers as soon as the guests arrive. I'll be in the kitchen for a few minutes. Meet me outside the door in ten. We'll greet guests as they arrive."

She nodded and twirled away. He watched her until she disappeared at the end of the room.

What had he been thinking when he agreed to this scheme?

When he told Sam, his friend had slapped his sides and howled like a hyena. "Thank God you were available," he'd said. "Otherwise who knows what guy she'd have collared. At least she's safe with you."

Zack wasn't so sure about the safe part. Tonight she looked gorgeous in a simple dress that hugged her body with soft, blue folds. Gold sandals wound up her ankles and showed off her perfect dancer's legs. She was a blue flame, sending off waves of heat whenever she moved. He was drawn to her like a man who'd been rescued from an ice floe.

Music—he thought it was a Gregorian chant—filled the room with subtle sounds, blending with the candlelit décor moments before the first guests arrived. Zack headed toward the door, hoping Mariel would appear soon. He wasn't sure how welcome he'd be among all these strangers.

"Deputy Dawg is here." Lane Brody sauntered over, another man trailing him. "I'm sorry, I don't recall your name."

Zack gave him his best death stare. "Zack Leoni."

Brody's companion squinted as if trying to place him. "Are you part of the security team, Mr. Leoni? I don't recall you."

"No. I'm Mariel's date."

"Really?" He snickered, poking Brody in the arm. "Guess you'll have to reassess your options, Lane. Your girl Mariel is taken."

"We'll see about that." Brody glanced at the door as Mariel returned and joined them.

"Mr. Cohen, how nice to see you. Have you met my

boyfriend, Zack?" She twined her fingers through Zack's and reached up to kiss him on the cheek. "He's been helping me set up."

"I'm sure everything is perfect, my dear." He smiled briefly and wandered inside. Brody followed. Zack was aware of poisonous looks aimed in his direction from the latter.

"How long do we have to stay?"

She looked up at him and batted her eyelashes. "Trying to get rid of me already?"

He ran his knuckles down her perfect cheek and leaned down to whisper in her ear. "Somebody's watching us. Want to give him something to think about?"

"What do you mean?"

He pulled her close and covered her lips with a consuming tenderness. She went rigid, but in a moment he felt her relax and lean into him, and that's when he deepened the kiss. He tilted his head for a better angle, moving his hands up into her loose hair, feeling her tremble against him. She was molten heat, the heart of a volcano, ready to consume him. If he let himself go, she'd be up against the wall and he'd be all over her, touching, kissing, wanting.

Back off. This is supposed to be an act.

He stepped back. His heart pounded in his ears. Their audience had turned toward the banquet room. The moment was over.

Mariel's chest swelled with each breath, her gaze locked on his face. She took a deep breath and moved out of reach. "Good job, Leoni. Time to go inside."

* * *

Mariel turned away and let the night air cool her. Weak knees still somehow held her upright while she went straight to the bar and picked up a glass of wine. She was giddy from the kiss. Her breasts felt heavy, her body longed for the next step as spikes of heat arrowed straight to her core.

She reminded herself this wasn't real. They were both playing a part. For a moment she'd lost herself in the kiss, the man. It probably wouldn't happen again.

Zack's hand stroking her shoulder didn't help.

She took a sip of wine and set it back on the bar. "I need to see what's going on in the kitchen. The appetizers should have been out by now."

His eyes and voice were soft. "Hurry back."

She escaped through the double doors. Instead of the kitchen, she ran into the ladies' room. Her body was on fire. How was she going to get through the next two weeks? It was torture to feel his palms on her skin, to see his gorgeous dimple when he smiled, to anticipate the brush of his lips on her mouth.

Zack was being charitable. He was repaying a debt he certainly didn't owe. It had been her decision to invite him into her bed all those years ago and he'd declined. Firmly.

And there's no reason to think he's changed his mind.

When she got herself back under control, Mariel returned to the banquet room, her mind focused on her job. Waiters emerged from the kitchen with trays of new potatoes stuffed with bleu cheese, and shrimp wrapped in bacon. Candlelight flickered from wall sconces. Cocktails and conversation flowed while guests nibbled and sipped. She exchanged a few words with the caterer, hand wrote a few clean up instructions on a large yellow pad, and left them in an alcove. Taking a deep breath, she made her way out to the dining area.

Scanning the room, she found Zack leaning toward a voluptuous redhead who'd cornered him near the bar. An emotion she didn't recognize rose in her, but she crushed it. He was hers for two weeks. After that…

He looked up and saw her, excused himself, and sauntered over. "Interesting people."

She nodded toward the doors as waiters moved into the kitchen with empty trays to pick up the first dinner course. Cohen shouted over the din, telling people to find their chairs.

"That's our cue to leave. Are you ready?"

Zack twined his fingers through hers and tugged her toward the door. "I was hoping you'd say that. This is definitely not my kind of party."

Pausing at the kitchen, she checked everything one last time. Satisfied, she nodded to the caterer and strode out the door.

"Can I take off my tie?"

She rolled her eyes, thinking he could take off everything if he wanted. "Sure. Your duties as official escort are over for the night."

"Not quite yet. I have to see you to your door. Maybe come in and check the closets. Make sure no bogeymen are hiding there."

She grimaced. "Did you have to say that?"

"Part of the service, ma'am. I promised Sam I'd take care of his favorite cousin."

"Sam is overprotective. All my relatives are. It's probably because I'm the youngest."

They got into the car and headed toward St. Helena.

"Want to stop somewhere for dinner? Those appetizers were pretty puny."

"It's summer. Hotels are full. Restaurants have waiting lists."

"It's Wednesday night."

"It's the Napa Valley."

"Fast food?"

She shook her head. "After you check the closets, you can stay for dinner. I think I have pizza in the freezer."

"For pizza, I'll even check under the bed."

She didn't want him anywhere near her bed unless he

was in it…with her.

They drove in comfortable silence—neither one needing to make idle conversation—and arrived in total darkness. That was odd. The porch light was on when she left. Maybe it burned out.

"The porch light is off."

"Are you sure you left it on? It was daylight when we left."

"I'm sure."

He frowned. "Give me your key and stay in the car."

"You think something's wrong?"

"Just being a cop."

"No, we'll go together."

Zack reached under the seat and grabbed a flashlight. "You can shine it on the door while I insert your key."

They reached the front door.

"It's open."

Zack pushed her behind him, took the flashlight, and moved the door inward inch by inch. Flashing the beam around the room, he reached over and switched on the interior light. He methodically checked every room, as he had done on Saturday night. The house was empty.

A tremor swept over her. Why was this happening?

"Come here." He folded her into his arms, gently stroking her back. "You're absolutely sure the lock engaged?"

"I think so." Her voice was muffled against his shoulder.

Pushing her gently away, he tilted her chin up so she had to look at him. "Let's make sure it wasn't a robbery. Start in the kitchen, then move to the other rooms in the house. Check on things like cell phones, computers, electronic devices, jewelry—the kinds of fast-turnover things thieves are usually after."

She wandered through the unit, opening cupboards and drawers, Zack behind her.

"The watch on top of the dresser is pretty valuable. It's still here."

Zack shook his head. "We can call this in to the local police, but if nothing's stolen, there's not much they can do." He paused, cocking his head. "You're one hundred percent sure you locked your door?"

Doubt clouded her mind. "Not one hundred percent."

On top of the tailgater and her anxiety about Lane, this was a nightmare. She always locked her door. And she was sure she'd turned on the porch light, even though it had still been daylight when they left.

Zack took her hand and she didn't pull away. She needed to touch someone.

"It was our first night in public as a couple. Maybe you were a little distracted and thought you'd locked the door and flipped on the light, but didn't."

She swallowed. Maybe he was right. She looked up at

him and shrugged. "Let's not call the police. Nothing's missing. I'll put the pizza in the oven."

"You don't possibly have any beer, do you?"

"Yes. But I work at a winery, and there's a bottle of their very best merlot is in the hall closet. Why don't we open it? We deserve something special."

Zack wandered over to the closet. A small wine refrigerator inside was half hidden by coats and jackets.

"Well, this is a surprise," he said.

She watched him take out the bottle and read the label before bringing it to the counter dividing the kitchen from the living room. There was a small table perched in an alcove for more formal meals, but the narrow counter had two stools, so guests could talk to her while she cooked.

Mariel opened the wine and poured it into an etched glass container. "Wine this good should be decanted to let the air open its flavors."

She poured it into two glasses, and came around the side of the counter to touch her glass against Zack's.

She tipped it and took a swallow, not even bothering to swirl it to let the "nose" introduce the bouquet before sipping fully. Zack gave it its due, letting the liquid dance on his tongue before swallowing.

"Wow, this is dynamite."

"It won a double gold rating at the fair."

"I can understand why."

She put down her glass and picked up her phone.

"What kind of music do you like?"

"I like all kinds of music, but I guess if I had to choose, I'd say I'm a country western guy. Keith Urban, Clint Black, Rascal Flats, all the good old boys."

"I like everything, too, but I'm more a fan of classical music. My mom loves jazz. Nana Reynoso adores Michael Jackson."

"Nana Reynoso likes Michael Jackson?"

"I'm surprised you didn't know."

"Haven't seen her in years, but I nearly suffered permanent loss of my taste buds from eating her chili at Sam's."

"She does overdo the peppers."

"When Sam and I helped her move into her condo a few years ago, it took us four hours to arrange all her furniture inside. She kept changing her mind about where she wanted the couch and the chair and the mirrors. Something about how shadows fall when the moon is full." Zack flexed his shoulders. "My arms still hurt thinking about it. I swear I heard coyote howling in the distance while we were hauling her furniture around."

Zack threw back his head and howled, then laughed, his eyes crinkling at the corners and his grin wide. The tickle in her stomach grew to a real, unladylike belly laugh. She couldn't help it. It had been a long time since she felt this comfortable with a man, but Zack could always make her laugh, even as a kid. When they got themselves under control, they gazed into each other's eyes. Something passed between them. Mariel wanted to inch forward until their lips met.

Not a good idea.

The timer went off and the smell of pizza filled the kitchen.

"It's time to eat, and I haven't made the salad." She grabbed a potholder, took the pizza out, and set it on empty burner on her stove to set up.

Zack was silent while she sliced the tomatoes and arranged them on top of a bed of romaine. After sprinkling croutons and parmesan cheese over the top, she set a bottle of Italian dressing next to the bowl.

Coming out of wherever his mind had gone, he joined her in the small kitchen space. "Here, I'll put the salad bowl on the table for you. "

"Great. Put the plates on, too. They're in the hutch against the wall. There should be napkins. Forks are in here."

Zack's movements were efficient while he set the table, a man at home in a kitchen. What a surprise. Mariel put the pizza on a hot plate and refilled their glasses.

"Mangiamo"

"Sounds like Italian to me."

"It is. It means 'let's eat.' "

Chapter 9

Few delights can equal the presence of
one whom we trust utterly.
--George MacDonald

Uncertainty faded into the background when the tall, muscular deputy sheriff was in her line of sight. His presence dominated the room, making everything in it look smaller. Mariel, taller than her two sisters, felt almost petite when standing beside him, although the top of her head reached a little above his shoulder.

She watched him eat with the precision he did everything else. His large hands with trimmed nails held the wineglass with care, as if it might break if he held it too tightly. He oozed power and control. She remembered those hands on her arms during self-defense training, hands she'd dreamed about having in other places.

Thoughts like that were dangerous.

"Would you like to have more salad?" She picked up the tongs and put them into the bowl, looking at him expectantly.

"No, I think this will do it for me."

He swallowed the last of his fifth piece of pizza, drained his glass, and took his plate to the sink to rinse it before putting it on the bottom rack of the dishwasher. His fork followed.

"I probably ought to be getting home."

Reluctant to let him go, Mariel followed him into the kitchen space and put water in the teakettle. What was wrong with her? Their relationship was false. Yet here she was, acting like a lovesick teenager, wanting to keep him here as long as she could.

"I don't want to overstay my welcome, but if you're going to make coffee, I think I will hang out a little longer."

"Oh, wonderful!" Mariel reached into a cupboard and brought out a coffee grinder and a French press.

"What's that thing?"

"It's a French coffee press. You crush the beans, put them in the press, pour hot water over them, and let them steep. Haven't you seen one before?"

"Can't say I have."

"I'm not much of a cook, but I make really good coffee."

She put water on to heat and placed a plate of her mother's chocolate chip cookies on the coffee table in front of the couch.

"Come over and have a cookie." She looked back over her shoulder as she set down her glass, accidentally catching the bottom on the edge of the plate.

"Oh, no." She jumped back as the glass tipped over and wine spattered on her hem.

Zack brought over napkins and she dabbed at the table, then her dress.

"I'm going to have to change and take care of this stain. Be right back. Turn off the water when it boils and pour it over the beans in the little pot."

It was heaven to slip on a T-shirt and yoga pants. She dabbed the spot on her dress with cold water before hanging it up in her shower, hoping the stain wouldn't set.

She picked up the wine-soaked napkin to put in the wastebasket.

What's this?

The remains of a filmy negligee lay at the bottom, its red silk folds torn and tossed away like a bloody rag. Someone with malicious intent had entered her house and rifled through her lingerie. An unseen hand had touched her most intimate garments.

Her stomach clenched. Everything would have to be washed. She couldn't stand the thought of wearing anything the intruder had handled.

Fighting nausea, she stumbled into the doorway. She held the tattered gown straight out in front of her like it was a dead fish.

Zack looked up. "What's wrong?"

She dropped the mangled silk in the doorway.

"Someone definitely came into my house and destroyed my nightgown. Someone's playing with me, Zack. I feel violated. I don't even want to stay here."

She bit back tears, determined not to let the asshole win. Zack's arms came around her, holding her close.

"Do you think Lane did this?"

"No. It's not his style."

"It's not the tailgater. I forgot to tell you, he's been cooling his heels in the county jail since yesterday."

Then who could it be? Mariel had always trusted people. She believed in their inherent goodness. It killed her to think someone out there wanted to inflict emotional pain. And it was working.

Her landline rang and she jumped.

"Do you have caller ID?" Zack asked.

"No."

"I'll answer it, then."

She saw him pick up the phone and listen before saying "hello."

"One moment." He handed her the phone. "It's a woman."

"Hello." Mariel's voice was weak, almost a whisper.

It was Jess. "Who answered the phone?"

"It's Zack. I had a break-in."

"Oh, my God. I can't believe this. When did it happen?"

"Tonight while I was at work."

There was a pause.

"I'd offer to come over, but I'm watching my sister's kids. I guess if Deputy Dreamy is there, you don't need me."

"Thanks for offering, but I'm going to be fine." If she told herself that over and over, it would be true. "What were you calling about?"

"I saw Lane last night. He…he couldn't stop talking about you."

"Rather insensitive of him, wasn't it?" Lane had dated Jess a few times before he spotted Mariel dancing at a party and launched his pursuit of her. He had discarded Jess like a bag of trash, even though Mariel had at first rebuffed him. He was a man who loved the chase, never caring who got hurt.

"He never was known for his tact," said Jess. "But we had a really good talk. I think he needed someone to listen to him. I can't believe he came to me."

"Don't be taken in by him. He's a user, and if he's being nice to you, he probably wants something."

"I think you're being a little hard on him, Mariel. He's

not a bad guy, although he did ask me about your new boyfriend."

"What did you tell him?"

"Not much. You've kept him a secret. Anyway, I'll let you get back to whatever you were doing. Will you be at work tomorrow?"

"I sure will. See you there."

She hung up and had no sooner put it on its stand when her cell rang. Not thinking, Mariel answered.

"Are you playing musical phones? What did you forget, Jess?"

There was silence until a menacing voice whispered her name. She whirled and handed Zack the phone, dropping it in his hand like a hot ember. Hands covering her mouth, she repeated the mantra in her head…you will not panic, you will not panic. Goose bumps cascaded over her while she watched Zack's expression change from calm interest to something else —his face was suffused with color and he gritted his teeth before he cut the connection.

"Why didn't you say anything?" Mariel's question came out in a squeak.

"It's better if the creep doesn't know I'm here." She saw him examine the numbers in her phone. "Do you recognize this number?"

She looked. "No."

He hesitated. "I'll take down the number and have it

checked out. Right now, I want you to report these incidents to the police."

She hesitated. "The nightgown wasn't worth much. I'd be wasting their time."

He held her shoulders and looked her in the eye. "Do it."

The car came quickly and a report was taken. She hoped the officer didn't think she was a nut case. She had a torn nightgown and a breather. But there was no real evidence of a break-in and nothing had been stolen. He left a card, telling her to call if any other incidents occurred, and went on his way.

Zack glanced at the clock on the wall. "It's late. I'd better be getting back."

She knew she was being selfish, but she didn't want him to go. The wind had whipped up, and she could hear it whistling through the trees.

"Can you stay with me Zack? Please."

She was aware of how awkward she sounded. But after what happened tonight, the thought of trying to sleep in her house alone overwhelmed her.

"Hey, lady, are you propositioning me again?" His tone was light as he tweaked the end of her nose, a smile playing at the corners of his mouth.

"Well, we know what kind of results that gets, don't we?"

He got a funny expression on his face, then nodded.

"I guess I can if it will make you feel better. Lord knows there's nobody at home waiting for me. And I don't like that someone was able to get in here while you were gone."

Mariel wasn't aware she'd been holding her breath. It came out in a whoosh, and the death grip tension had on her shoulders eased a bit.

"Thank you."

* * *

What was he thinking? He was no bodyguard. He was in law enforcement, but guarding that body? He must be out of his mind.

Sam would chew my ass if he found out I spent the night here.

Or would he?

Zack was supposed to help Sam take care of his cousin. Fat chance. He wasn't even sure he could trust himself around her.

"Are you sure about this?"

"I'm a wimp. I don't want to be alone tonight."

He sat down again and held her hand. "Is there someone else you can stay with? Your friend Jess?"

"She's babysitting at her sister's house."

"How about your grandmother?"

She squeezed his hand and bit her lip, then nodded. "Okay, I'll call Nana Reynoso and see if she's awake."

He picked up the cell phone she'd left on the table.

Handing it to her, he slanted a glance at her trembling hand. She was terrified, and it wrenched his heart to see it.

She punched in a number and held the phone to her ear. After a few seconds she left a message and ended the call, looking up at him, her eyes wide.

"She didn't pick up. She must be asleep."

"How about your parents?"

"No, I don't want to worry them."

He grinned. "Well then, I guess you're stuck with me."

He tested the couch and found it to be adequate. His long legs would hang over the end, but his tour in Afghanistan had proven he could sleep anywhere. Mariel brought out a pillow, a folded sheet and a couple of blankets. She stacked the linens on a chair and plopped down next to him, a full glass of wine in her hand. She'd filled his glass previously, but he was starting to feel pretty mellow, so he declined another pour and opted for the coffee cooling on the stove.

Curling her feet under her, she turned to face him on the couch.

"So how long have you been a deputy?"

"Six months."

"Did you always want to be a cop? I thought you'd become a veterinarian. You were always bringing home strays."

Some of his tension melted at the memory. "I did have quite a menagerie."

"But you changed your mind?"

He shook his head, recalling his pipe dream days. "I thought I was good enough to play professional football. When I graduated from college and realized it wasn't going to happen, I came back here, enrolled in the sheriff's academy and started working as a deputy. Then my Army Reserve unit was called up, and I shipped out."

Her eyes softened. "Were you terribly disappointed about not playing football?"

He grinned. "Let's just say I had an inflated view of my talents then, thinking four years of college football with two winning seasons was enough to get me to the NFL. It was a good reality check. What about you? Last I heard you wanted to be a professional dancer."

Her face lit with an adorable smile. "Since we are owning up to our faults, I will confess as well. I tried out for 'So You Think You Can Dance.' Shot down in the first round."

"You're a good dancer."

"The judges didn't think so. I was terribly upset. I wanted to prove my worth, to show my family I could be as successful as Lindsay and Paige. When I failed, I meekly signed up for the next semester at the community college. It's what my parents wanted me to do."

Her face looked sad, he wanted to wipe her hurt away. "I don't know why you think you aren't as good as your sisters. I know both of them, and they're different, but not better. You're unique, Mariel. You know how to make people feel important. It's a gift."

She sipped her wine and reached for a cookie. "I think you're the one who knows how to make people feel important, Zack. But thank you. Do you want to see if there's something on TV?"

"No, I like talking to you."

He looked over at her, curled up on the couch, a glass of wine in her hand. Cookie crumbs fell on her lap, and she brushed them off with one hand after popping the last bite into her mouth. She stopped chewing, swallowed, and stared at him, her eyes widening as if seeing him for the first time. Heat flared in his groin. He couldn't stand it any longer. He reached for her glass and set it down on the table. Moving over, he put his hand on the back of her head and leaned into her, kissing her gently, tasting chocolate and merlot.

She sighed as he deepened the kiss, running his tongue along the inside of her mouth as if mapping territory. Her hair was soft and he bunched a handful in his fist while wrapping his free hand around her back. This was so wrong, so selfish…and so damn good.

Her whimper nearly undid him. He slid her onto his

lap—awkwardly at first—then situated her over his knees. She opened her mouth under his while her fingers worked at the buttons of his shirt. Soft hands slid up and down his chest, melting his defenses.

Damn.

He broke the kiss, gently slipped out from under her, and stood. With his back to her, he reached down and adjusted his pants.

"Look Mariel. I think this is a bad idea. You're reacting to a serious scare, and I'm supposed to be protecting you. I'm sorry."

He used his deputy voice, the one that made him remember he was a responsible adult who didn't take advantage of frightened women needing comfort. He tried to picture Mariel as a pesky teen with thin silver bands on her teeth. No images came to him. All he could see was the gorgeous woman with long-lashed eyes and full, pouting lips. The memory of her soft curves was branded on his chest. He wanted to strip off her clothes and grab handfuls of her and kiss her until she squirmed and gasped for air. He wanted to lay her on the couch and dip his fingers in her wine glass and sprinkle droplets of merlot on her body and lick them off.

She'd taste so good.

"You are protecting me." Her voice brought him out of his reverie and he turned to see her looking hurt and huggable at the same time. "Your being here means I can sleep in my own house tonight without putting a chair against the door or leaving all the lights on. But it doesn't mean we have to keep each other at arm's length. Maybe you don't find me attractive, but if you say so, I'll call you a liar. I know what I felt when I sat in your lap."

He took a long, deep, steadying breath. He needed to reply, but he was afraid his voice would shake.

"Of course I find you attractive, but there are things about me you don't know." *Maybe I'm someone you won't want around once you find out what a loser I am.*

"I do know you, Zack." She sounded breathless, sexy. She was killing him. "You're my hero."

He stared at her. "I'm no hero, Mariel."

"But you are." She patted the couch next to her. "Come back."

He sat down, her scent wrapping around him again in a sensual cloud. Moving to the other end of the couch would be juvenile. He picked up her hand, idly stroking her fingers one at a time, willing his heartbeats to slow.

"Remember the parking lot behind the gym at the high school, the one that was dark because the lights were always burned out?"

"Yeah. I kept a little flashlight in my gym bag so I could find my car on dark nights."

"One night you came out of the locker room when

two guys were harassing me while I waited for Sam. I was about fourteen, and I'd decided to catch a ride with Sam instead of Paige."

"I remember. You were fighting off a couple of bullies. One of them was trying to feel you up."

"You pulled me free, confronted them, and they both ran off." Her fingers twined with his.

He'd been furious. At them, at her, at her cousin Sam, who was still dawdling in the locker room. She shouldn't have been left in the dark alone.

She tugged at him, unfurling her legs so she could scoot closer. Her eyes were bright and trusting, drawing him into their emerald depths. When she parted her lips and climbed back into his lap, he was lost.

Chapter 10

*"Trust in yourself. Your perceptions are
often far more accurate
 than you are willing to believe."*
--Claudia Black

Mariel moved her bottom, and got instant confirmation that he still wanted her. Relief rolled through her.

He kissed her open-mouthed, and her world narrowed until nothing existed but the heat between them. His lips were firm, demanding no more of her than she was willing to give. She sighed as the kiss deepened and their tongues twined until she was weak with need. She wanted more. She wanted it all.

The fingers of his free hand reached under her shirt to stroke her. His mouth was hot, and she wanted it where his fingers touched. Breathing hard, she broke the kiss and fumbled with his shirt, pulling it open to rub her hands across his muscular chest.

His lips were on her neck, his breath warm against her ear. His hands reached behind to unfasten the piece of cloth that kept their skin from touching. Need pooled in her core as it came loose and she lifted the edges of her shirt so she could rub against him.

She shifted and arched, anticipating the feel of his lips on her body.

Her cell phone rang.

Startled they pulled apart. Fear curled in her gut, replacing the desire that consumed her moments before. Fighting for breath, she refastened her clothes.

Zack grabbed the cell from the table and handed it to her.

"Do you recognize this number?"

She looked at it like it was a snake, before taking it from him and looking at the number.

She took a deep breath, trying to bring herself under control.

"Hi, Nana."

"What's wrong? You sound like you've been running."

She felt like a piece of cooked spaghetti. "I'm fine."

"Is there a man there?"

"Why do you think that? Did you hear a coyote in the night? Did a crow peck at your window?"

"No an owl brought me a message. Dropped it right on my windshield. Actually, I'm outside your house and there's a strange car in the driveway."

Mariel looked out the front window. A vintage Cadillac with fins was parked out front, the glow of a cigarette visible through the window.

Zack re-buttoned his shirt. "Who is it?"

"It's my grandmother."

"Well, are you going to invite me in, or make me sit out here in the dark?" Nana was never one to mince words.

"Come in. I have beer."

"Well that's a blessing."

Nana flounced in carrying an overnight bag. A much tidier Zack went to the refrigerator, opened a beer, and handed it to her. She looked him up and down.

"Nice. Much better than the last one." She hesitated. "Do I know you?"

"Nana." Mariel felt a blush staining her cheeks. "What are you doing here this time of night?"

"I got your message and I heard fear in your voice. So I came to spend the night with you." She glanced at the bedding in the chair. "Your sisters are right. You've got the sight, too. I see you're already prepared."

She looked slyly at Zack, who grinned back. "Hi. I'm Zack Leoni."

"Sam's friend? The one who helped arrange my furniture? Still play football?"

"No. I'm a deputy sheriff now."

She stepped back. "Oh."

Mariel couldn't help herself. "What's the matter, Nana? Your license expired?"

"Ha. Ha. Funny girl. I'll go put my stuff in your bedroom, and you can say good night." She walked past the couch, pausing at the bedroom door to pick up the torn nightgown Mariel had dropped earlier. She shook her head. "I'll take this with me."

Mariel sighed and nodded toward Zack. "I'll walk you out."

They paused at his car and he opened the door. "How old is she?"

"Nobody knows, and nobody asks."

He tugged her into his arms. She felt like nothing in the world could hurt her as long as her hero was here. His finger stroked her cheek and he looked into her eyes before kissing her gently.

"Hey, girlfriend. What time do you get off tomorrow?"

"I can get off early. Why?"

"Time for another lesson in self-defense. I want you to feel safe, especially after tonight."

She smiled. "I feel perfectly safe when you're with me."

His brows furrowed. "But I can't be with you all the time. I want you to know how to protect yourself when you're on your own."

"See you tomorrow, then."

* * *

Zack pulled into traffic, wanting nothing more than to go home and feel cold water drawing the heat out of his body. He'd lost control tonight, but God, she was addictive.

He rolled the window down and let the air stream over his face.

Turning onto Highway 29, he drove past vineyards and darkened wineries. A few restaurants still had cars in their lots. Turning onto Trinity Road, the car climbed and twisted around hairpin turns until he reached his driveway and the sanctuary of his home.

He slept soundly and woke up the next morning to the ringtone of his cell phone.

"Good, you're up. Come outside."

Some days, he decided later, the gods look down on mere mortals and grant them a crumb or two of their heavenly bounty. It was his training officer.

"I wanted you to be the first to know. The wife of the guy who's accusing you called the station right before I went off duty. She made an appointment to come in Sunday. She's changing her story, and she's going to tell the truth. Maybe she's tired of being a punching bag, but more likely she's doing it for her son."

"How's the kid doing?"

"Still in a coma."

"Sorry to hear that."

Zack unclenched his fists, relief settling on his shoulders. Maybe he'd be exonerated. He'd still face a disciplinary hearing for not following procedure, but the brutality charge might go away if the wife stood up for him. No one in their right mind could believe he'd hurt a kid. Ever.

He couldn't stop grinning.

He wouldn't have to resign. He could get on with his life. He'd have time to really think about his future.

He could pursue Mariel.

After catching up on office news, Zack went back in the house. He brewed a pot of coffee, made his weekly call to his parents in Oregon, then went over his list of projects for the day. He and Mariel could fit in another self-defense session. The last one had nearly done him in, but he wanted her to be confident in her ability to escape an attacker.

The break-in and the phone breather still disturbed him. She said it wasn't Brody, but she also said he played mind games. Maybe he asked someone to do it as a joke…a little power trip.

If she left her door unlocked, anyone could have gone inside. His gut told him it was someone with a key.

Who had one?

Last night their relationship had moved to a new level. If Nana Reynoso hadn't shown up, there would have been a different outcome, one that would have brought closure to the humiliating scene of five years ago. He still owed her a more thorough explanation and was eager to deliver it.

And take her up on the offer he'd rejected, if she'd have him. Maybe make this boyfriend thing real.

After the session at Sam's, maybe she'd like to go to dinner.

He knew the perfect place.

Chapter 11

Trust is the first step to love.
--Munshi Premchand

Mariel peered into her closet. Her red sundress would be perfect for an outdoor restaurant. After their workout, Zack had invited her to dinner, but he hadn't given her any more information except he was picking her up at seven.

The new self-defense session had gone well, even with Sam hovering in the background. Basic moves she'd learned last time were firmly locked in her memory. After the incidents of the past week, she felt more secure in her ability to get away from an attacker.

Her growing feelings for Zack were another matter. Even with Sam watching, her awareness of Zack jangled her senses. Every touch, ever brush of their bodies made her tingle in sensitive places. She was ready to throw caution to the wind and give in to the throb that pulsed in the lower part of her body.

Her cell pinged with a message.

It was Zack. "Wear jeans and a warm jacket. See you in fifteen."

What is he, a mind reader?

She put the dress back on its hanger and put on a pair of fitted jeans and her cashmere sweater. Slipping into the bathroom she checked her makeup and dabbed a light perfume behind her ears.

If this was a date, it was casual, and she loved the idea. Zack was a beer and chips kind of guy, not pretentious like some of the men she'd met in her business. Although she'd known him for a long time, he'd changed in subtle ways. She couldn't put her finger on it, but she thought it might be confidence. He walked into a room like he owned it, like he had a purpose for being there. Taking charge seemed to come easy for him.

How she envied him. Making decisions and sticking to them had been hard for her to learn, and she still struggled at times. It wasn't simply the result of too many years of other people making decisions for her. She was spontaneous, rather than analytical. She liked to get going and get things done, which sometimes resulted in unexpected outcomes.

The roar of a motorcycle broke into her musings. She

peered out the window in time to see Zack park his Harley.

We're going somewhere on the Harley?

She opened the door and he stood there in his leathers, looking like the hero of a bad boy film. His eyes sparkled, and a shock of hair had slipped down over his forehead. He held up two helmets.

"Ready?"

"We're going on the motorcycle?"

"Yup." His glance swept her body, focusing on her high-heeled sandals. "You look great, but I'd recommend a pair of boots."

"Have a seat while I change."

She dug out a pair of calf-high boots, switched her lightweight jacket for a heavier one, dropped her cell into her pocket, and went back into the living room.

"Any problems today?"

"No."

She locked her door and tugged at the handle to make sure. Anticipation bubbled through her as she turned and studied the bike. It was a real black and chrome beauty. Zack wouldn't put her in danger. And she'd always wanted to try riding.

"Ever been on Sam's?"

"Are you serious? He wouldn't let me touch it."

Zack chuckled and handed her a helmet. "You need to put this on. It will probably muss your hair."

She took it and set it down on the sidewalk. Taking a scrunchie out of her pocket, she secured her hair into a low mass at the back of her neck, then put the helmet on. She expected it to be heavy, but it wasn't.

"You get on first, then I'll climb on in front when the bike is level. Wrap your arms around my waist or use the handles on the sides of the seat. Then follow my lead. If I lean one way, you lean in the same direction. Got it?"

"I guess so."

"Are you afraid?"

Was she? She heard about accidents all the time, but Sam said motorcycles were safe if the operator knew what he was doing and was aware of his surroundings. Zack's focus was legendary…especially when he'd played football.

You experienced a bit of it last night, too, didn't you? The memory heated her cheeks while she got on the bike as directed.

"No. Excited."

"Let's go."

She climbed onto the bike, and when he seated himself, she slipped her arms around him and snuggled against his back. Her seat was surprisingly comfortable, but the man was, too.

I could get used to this.

They left the main highway and wound along back

roads through vineyards to the Silverado Trail, a road that had almost as many wineries as the main highway through the Napa Valley. Every nerve ending responded to the exhilaration of the wind blowing over her, the scenery flying by, and the warmth of Zack's muscular body in front of her.

A narrow, paved road led through rows of bright green vineyards in full leaf with new clusters of grapes growing below their trellises. It curved up a slope, and when they reached the top, Zack stopped the bike near a tree. He helped Mariel climb off and took a large bundle out of one saddlebag and a light blanket out of the other.

The view across the valley was spectacular, and the sun was only now beginning to set. "What is this place?"

Zack grinned and spread the blanket.

"Remember when I got that summer job right out of high school as a cellar worker?"

"You mean cellar rat. As I recall, your job was to clean barrels and fill orders for wine club clients."

"Busted." He cocked his head in that endearing way she remembered. "This was my favorite place in the world in those days. This vineyard is still owned by that winery, and they know I come up here sometimes."

She smirked. "You bring lots of girls up here, do you?"

His smile faded, and his intent look sent shock waves through her. "No, Mariel. You're the first one."

She held his gaze and they both inched closer. Was he thinking about last night? The memory of his lips on her mouth, her neck, and—if only Nana had waited a few more seconds—her body made her ache in all her secret places. She wanted him to kiss her now, while the sunset glowed orange behind them, and the valley lights began to twinkle like diamonds sprinkled on a net.

He was every girl's naughty wish wrapped in leather and temptation, and she wanted him in the worst way.

An owl hooted in the tree above them, breaking the mood.

Mariel licked her lips and dragged her gaze to the view of the valley and the hills against the western sky.

"The view is spectacular."

"Yes, it is." She slanted a glance at him, but he was looking at her, not the sunset.

"What's in the bag?"

"Our dinner."

He took out a box of thin crackers, a package of sliced cheeses, a small container of assorted olives, and a package of chicken tenders. They sat with the food between them while he opened a half bottle of merlot from Mariel's winery.

"A glass for you, but only a few sips for the driver. Hope you don't mind?"

"Of course not, Zack." She spread her arms wide, palms open and embracing the view, the meal, the stars —everything. "This is wonderful."

They ate in silence, watching the sunset fade into darkness. It was warm, and crickets chirped rapidly, filling the night with soft sounds. When they finished, Zack wrapped up the containers and put them back in the saddlebag.

Mariel lay back on the blanket, watching the stars come out until Zack joined her.

"So many stars. They seem brighter up here."

His hand crept over and he laced his fingers with hers. "They are, because there aren't any lights."

He had strength in his hands, but gentleness, too. She remembered a fawn he rescued when the mother deer was killed by a car. He'd held the orphan carefully, keeping it warm while she and Keira called the Animal Rescue League.

"What are you thinking about?"

"I'm remembering that orphaned deer you found."

He turned. "What made you think of that?"

"Your hands…strong, but gentle. The way you are. You gave up a lot to take care of your little sister. We were always hanging around when you probably wanted to be alone."

He reached over and kissed her nose.

"I liked having you guys around. Especially you. I had

such a crush on you when I was a kid."

"No way. I had a crush on you, too."

"I know."

"Then why didn't you…"

"…act on it?" He reached over and pulled off the scrunchie with one hand, letting her hair loose around her shoulders. "Age difference. It mattered more when we were younger. And Sam. He would have killed me. I didn't want to risk losing him as a friend. Even for you. He was—is—the brother I never had."

His fingers stroked her cheek, and she wanted to wrap her arms around him and pull him down to her. But the intimacy of the mood kept her quiet. There was more she wanted to know.

"Did you still have a crush on me the night of the talent show?" She was ready to hear the truth.

"Oh, yeah. I hadn't seen you in a long time, but I kept in touch with Sam when I was out of state during my last two years of college. He liked to talk about family. I knew what was going on with his brothers and with you and your sisters. When I saw you, my feelings came rushing back. You'd changed. You were still funny and vivacious, but you had a serious side, too. And you'd grown into the kind of woman guys dream about."

His free hand played in her hair, moving long strands over her shoulders. The gentle tugging was like a soothing massage.

Then why? Why did you say what you said?"

"Because I had to report for duty the next day, was shipping out the next week ,and already knew I was being deployed overseas. It wasn't a time to begin something so important. But, God help me, I wanted to. I wanted you like I'd never wanted anything in my life. Plus, you were willing and available and you'd taken the initiative."

"The 'not being into you' statement hurt, Zack. Even without the live microphones."

"I was so surprised, it was the first thing that came into my head. Afterward, I hated myself for not saying something more like, 'let's talk about this later,' or not replying at all. I've owed you an apology for years. Will you accept it now?"

She sat up and retrieved her glass of merlot. Dipping her finger in it, she traced his lips, then leaned up and kissed him. "Are you into me now?"

"Do stars fill the sky tonight?" His voice was low and his half-closed eyes studied her through his long lashes while that shock of unruly hair fell over his forehead. Desire so strong it nearly choked her flickered to life in her core.

This was a man she'd wanted for years, and this time he wasn't going to get away.

* * *

He'd chosen this place because the night was warm and

the moon was almost full. He'd often thought about bringing a girl here, but he didn't want to share his special place with a casual hookup. She had to be important to him...special.

Mariel is special, and I've wanted her for a long, long time.

He lay back on the blanket and held his breath while she took off her sweater. He'd known she had lush curves, but that body was spectacular. Next she took off her boots...one at a time...then wriggled out of her jeans, revealing a thin piece of matching lace. When she straddled him and reached down to lick the remaining merlot from his lips, he thought he'd die on the spot.

"You have on too many clothes, Zack." Her breath was warm against his ear.

"I can fix that, but if I do, you'll have to get off and I don't want you off. I like this view."

Her breasts pressed into his chest as she leaned down and gave him a searing kiss, her hair tickling his face. She unbuttoned his shirt and spread it away from his body. Soft kisses followed.

He wanted to feel her skin against his own, and there was only one way to do that. He wrapped his arms around her and rolled her onto her back, so he was on top.

"Like to be in control, do you?"

"Always have."

Those beautiful red lips curled into a sexy smile while she watched him take off the rest of his clothes and lie back down on the blanket. He turned on his side so he could stroke her. "Now you have on too many clothes."

Her hand moved over his abs while he kissed her, open-mouthed. She reached between them and unfastened her bra in the front, letting it fall to her sides. He inhaled sharply. She was as beautiful as he'd imagined. He let his fingers skim over her body, watching the play of emotions on her face. She closed her eyes and moaned softly.

He pulled her against him and threw a leg over her. She squirmed with need, trying to get even closer.

He kissed her again, moving to the pulse point at her throat, her shoulder, the curve of her breast.

"Am I still a little girl?"

"You're all woman."

She was breathless, her voice shaky. "Then get on with it, Leoni."

He reached over to pull a foil wrapper out of his jeans pocket. "I've been waiting for a long time, Mariel."

"So have I."

The moon rose, right on cue, when he slipped off the last piece of Mariel's clothing and settled in to make this a night she'd always remember, to wipe away the humiliation of the past.

When her cries of pleasure broke the silence of the

night, he knew he'd succeeded.

Chapter 12

You must trust and believe in people or
life becomes impossible.
--Anton Chekhov

Friday nights were busy at the Teen Club. Parents were in and out. Craft classes were underway. Rubber soles squeaked on the basketball floor followed by shouts of triumph when a basket made it through the hoop.

Mariel leaned back in the hard metal chair. She'd finished teaching her dance class an hour ago and was happy to sit down, even if it was in a smelly gym. The corridor along the wall of the gymnasium was the main thoroughfare into the rest of the building. It was the best place to set up a table for ticket sales.

"Tell me again what we're doing here?" Jess shoved back her chair and uncrossed her legs, standing to stretch.

"We're impressing our boss by volunteering at his favorite charity in Sonoma Valley."

"You teach a class here. What am I doing here?"

Mariel laughed. "You're helping your best friend sell tickets to the winery's annual charity event."

The annual fund-raiser was coming together nicely. She'd found two bands willing to donate their time, and three chocolatiers to provide desserts at cost. The owners had decided the proceeds would go to Michael Callahan's family to pay for his medical expenses. Michael's father was a personal trainer and Mr. Cohen was acquainted with him. He was also a member of the Teen Center Board.

"Hot date last night? You look wrung out." Jess's tone dripped sarcasm.

Mariel looked up sharply. She sometimes wondered if Jess resented her. When Lane had dropped Jess, she'd been hurt. But that was in the past. Jess couldn't still be in love with him, although she hadn't dated anyone since.

Mariel reminded herself Jess wasn't the only one who hadn't dated. The closest she'd come to any kind of date was with Zack and it had all been for show until the night he agreed to stay with her.

And then there was last night.

Last night was special and too new to share. She hadn't even wrapped her mind around her feelings yet, so she remained quiet.

"I've been too busy with the fund-raiser."

"Oh. I thought maybe you and Deputy Dreamy had something going. You always jump right into the fire, don't you, Mariel?"

"What's that supposed to mean?"

"Nothing. It's just that you always seem to have guys panting after you."

She must have shown her annoyance at the sarcastic comments because Jess looked apologetic. "Hold the fort for a while. I'll find us some coffee."

When Jess came back she was her usual bright, chatty self. She put the cup down next to the signup sheet for the party. "Are you dancing? You could offer a few lessons in Flamenco as an auction prize."

"I don't perform in public anymore. The kids do it."

"You *are* the one in charge of the fundraiser. Don't you want it to be successful?"

"I like to plan parties, not *be* the party."

"Your hot little flamenco dance at the Christmas party last year certainly made a few guys drool."

The snarky Jess was back. What was the matter with her today?

Mariel thought back to the party. She hadn't wanted to perform, but Mr. Cohen had insisted once he heard about her talent. She could still feel Lane's hot gaze following her. She wouldn't do it again.

The noise level increased behind her as a buzzer sounded, ending the basketball game. Mariel glanced at the signup sheet in front of her. Sixty names for the fund-raiser. They'd need a lot more, but she was sure the winery owners would match what was brought in.

She picked up her cup in both hands to warm her icy fingers and sipped the fragrant liquid, feeling it slide down her throat. The smell of sweaty gym socks reminded her she had laundry to do at home.

She'd left her cell phone in the car and found it loaded with messages. Most were work, but one was from her mother.

"Lindsay and Chris get back tomorrow. Your father is digging a pit to roast a pork butt in the ground. Can you come? I could use some help with the sides."

"Sure. What time?"

"Four o'clock should do it."

"Is it okay if I bring someone?"

"Is it your friend Jess? She's always welcome."

"No, Mama. It's a man."

There was a pause. "Your grandmother said there was someone at your house a few nights ago."

Why did she feel defensive around her mother? "What did she tell you?"

"She said you were feeling scared from your bad experience and she went over to spend the night. She didn't say who the man was. Is that who you want to bring?"

"It was Zack. I had him over for dinner." She hesitated. "As a thank-you."

"You can bring anyone you like, Mariel, but are you sure you want to bring the man who humiliated you at that talent show?"

"I'm totally over that old incident now, and I'm sure no one will remember it." Her sisters would raise their eyebrows, but they wouldn't say anything. Nor would Papa.

She hadn't told anyone about the break-in except her grandmother. Apparently Nana had decided to keep it to herself, letting Mama think she was still worried about the tailgater.

She didn't realize she'd been tense until she put down the phone and felt her shoulders relax. Now all she had to do was convince Zack. Sam was invited. Zack would feel at home, and they didn't have to mention their "fake" relationship. No outsiders would be there, only family members. They wouldn't have to lie.

Sam knew about their little charade, but wouldn't say anything. He should be pleased that she and Zack were seeing each other for real. He'd always kept an eye out for her, making sure she stayed out of trouble. Now she was in a relationship with his best friend. She could hardly wait to tell him.

Were they really, or was last night a natural response to

the mood and the moonlight?

Mariel sat in her car and mulled it over. The kisses they'd shared were mutual. She'd wanted him in the worst way. And he'd not only responded, but had taken charge.

Her body purred at the memory.

She was the bold one, the one who chased and initiated. He was the one who usually pulled away. But last night he'd arranged the picnic and the ensuing seduction. Maybe he was starting to care.

Or it might have been a one-night stand.

An old memory crept into her consciousness. She'd sneaked into his room when he was doing homework one afternoon and snatched the papers off his desk, running out the door. She did it so he'd chase her, wrestle her to the ground, and take them back. She'd stolen a kiss, and he made a face, pretending he was disgusted. But the grin afterward and the softness in his eyes told her otherwise. She'd had such a crush on him then.

She had more than a crush on him now.

Zack didn't answer when she called, so she left a message, giving him the time and date of the family barbecue. She hoped he'd come. It was time she had a boyfriend who was dependable, and there was nobody more dependable than Zack.

* * *

Zack parked his bike in the driveway and strode toward the front door. Music drifted on the breeze, and laughter carried clear into the street. He recognized the sound of Sam trying to sing to a popular song. The man couldn't carry a tune to save his life. He hadn't told Sam he'd be here, but he could handle Sam.

And he couldn't wait to see Mariel again.

No one came to the door, so he went around to the side and let himself in through the gate. The smell of roasted pork made his stomach growl. Three picnic tables lay end-to-end and were loaded with bowls of chips, salsa and guacamole. Smoke curled into the sky from the barbecue pit set in the farthest part of the back garden.

He scanned the group and nodded at several Reynoso cousins. Sam spotted him and sauntered over, a beer in hand. "I didn't know you would be here. Glad to see you." He guided him over to a cooler full of beer, white wine, and soft drinks on ice and lowered his voice. "So how are things going? Has Brody ridden his horse out of town yet? Is the charade over?"

He spied Mariel by the food table. "I think we have another week before he leaves."

Mariel set down a big bowl of potato salad, the corners of her mouth quirking up in a pleased expression. She wore jeans and a plaid shirt that molded to her perfect body, and her hair was in two long braids.

She looked adorable.

"You came. I wasn't sure if you would." She leaned up and kissed him on the cheek, leaving her hand on his arm.

Sam frowned.

Too bad.

"Couldn't pass up this invitation. I get tired of my own cooking."

Mariel linked her arm in his and steered him toward Lindsay and Chris. Zack felt Sam's confused stare even with his back turned.

After meeting Mariel's new brother-in-law, he congratulated the couple on their marriage. Mariel tugged him away and filled him in on their history.

Next they moved to another group, where Paige was the center of attention. He knew Paige. They'd been in a couple of classes together in high school.

Paige turned and smiled. "Zack, how nice to see you. This is my husband, Jake Madison." They shook hands and talked about viticulture in the Mayacamas area. When Paige and Jake's new house was built, they'd practically be neighbors.

Zack was enjoying himself. Mariel still had her arm linked in his, while Sam's gaze still followed their progress. When they turned toward the barbecue pit, Zack halted. A man with a floppy hat and long-handled shovel tended the coals, his gaze fixed on Zack. Two men who resembled him stood nearby.

Zack looked down, thinking he must have spilled something on his shirt. Or worse, maybe he had given one of them a ticket.

"Come on, Zack. It's time to introduce you to Papa." Mariel's sunny face made his apprehension dissolve.

He stuck out his hand, grasping the callused one offered by Mariel's father.

"Glad you came. Wanted to thank you for what you did."

"I'm glad I was home. Sometimes I pull the night shift."

The man nodded and went back to tending the fire.

Zack knew from Sam that Pedro Reynoso was a man of few words, so he wasn't bothered when Mariel pulled him in yet another direction. "Come on. There's one more person to meet."

"What are you, the family social director?"

"I'm a professional. I help people mingle for a living." She was obviously in her element. And she was having fun. Zack wanted to laugh he felt so good, but he didn't want her to think he was laughing at her. He was amused, charmed, and maybe even enchanted by this engaging creature who hauled him around like he was the guest of honor instead of Chris and Lindsay.

"I'd really like to sit down for a few minutes," he said, planting his feet and pointing to the appetizer-laden tables. "Preferably over there."

"But Sam is over there, and he's been glaring at us since you arrived."

"That's because you've been treating me like a boyfriend."

She stood directly in front of him and put her hands on his shoulders. "Aren't you?"

Her mouth relaxed in a seductive expression that made his insides feel like melted marshmallows. Here they were, in the middle of the Reynoso's back yard, surrounded by her aunts, uncles, and cousins, and all he wanted to do was lean down and cover those luscious lips with his own.

"I dare you," she whispered. Her eyes sparkled with mischief.

He wanted to, but instead he tugged at her braid.

"Mariel, come help with the beans." A woman's voice summoned her from the back porch. Mariel turned and waved at a woman in a white apron, who stood with her arms folded. Zack guessed she was Mariel's mother.

"Go ahead. I'll shoot the breeze with Sam and grab some guacamole."

She strode off in the direction of the kitchen. Zack watched her, his focus on her tight, gorgeous little butt, knowing he had a silly grin on his face and not caring who saw it. He loved watching her walk, almost on her toes. A dancer. Maybe she would dance for him.

Time to face the firing squad.

Sam joined Zack at the table. "You two sure are friendly."

"You know I've been helping her with a problem."

"Yeah? Looks like maybe you're creating a different one."

"Lay off, Sam. It's not what you think."

"You two look pretty tight to me."

Zack ignored Sam and dumped a few tortilla chips onto a paper plate. Someone strummed a guitar over by the barbecue pit. It was a peaceful afternoon in a Napa neighborhood. Not a time to be arguing with his best friend.

Sam leaned against the picnic table, his arms folded, waiting for an explanation. Zack flexed his shoulders, popped a chip into his mouth, and grinned.

"I like her. A lot. I admit it."

Sam shook his head. "I like her, too. But we're supposed to be watching out for her, steering her clear of trouble. You look at her like a starving man looks at a feast. You, my friend, are not what she needs right now. You're facing some serious shit. If you get involved with her, you'll break her heart. And trust me, it's been broken so many times I'm surprised anything is left."

"I'll be careful with her. I promise."

Zack watched Sam walk away. He wanted to call him back and tell him about Mrs. Callahan changing her statement. Yeah, he'd have to face a disciplinary action for losing his cool, but he wouldn't be booted out in disgrace or worse, put in jail.

"You look like you've lost your best friend." Nana Reynoso, decked out in a one-piece black jumpsuit with gold chains around her neck and matching gold flip-flops, held up the guacamole bowl. Zack scooped a bit on his chip and chewed carefully while Sam disappeared into the house.

"You may be right."

Nana put the bowl back on the table and picked up her beer.

"Sam's a good boy. But he's a control freak. He has to be in charge of everyone and everything. You, of all people, should know that. You played football with him when he was the captain of the team. Didn't he try to tell the quarterback what plays to make?"

"Yup, he also thought he was the coach."

Nana nodded, gold hoops bobbing from her ears. "See…you do know him." She took a bite of a taquito and grimaced. "Frozen. Paige must have brought these. The girl can't cook worth a damn."

Nana Reynoso might be the family character, but she had a way of putting people at ease. Right when he thought the conversation was going well, she brought up the one subject he'd hoped to avoid. "Now, about my granddaughter."

He took the bait. "What about her?"

"She's a pretty girl and men gravitate to her. She's made a lot of bad choices in her short life. Lane Brody was one of them."

He sat down and looked thoughtfully at the one person in Mariel's family who knew about the harassing phone call and the break-in at Mariel's condo. "Do you think he's the one behind her current set of problems?"

"Not his style. It would take too much effort, and he's the type who wants other people to work hard on his behalf. He wouldn't lower himself. It's someone else. Someone right under our nose. Someone who wants to scare her, but not hurt her."

"Any ideas?"

"A few. But my crystal ball tells me she's going to figure this out by herself."

"You have a crystal ball?"

"Sure. I've got tea leaves and a broom, too. What I don't have is a fresh beer. Do you think you could bring me another one?" She batted her eyelashes at him.

Zack laughed and obliged, bringing back a Budweiser and putting it on the table. "Here you go. Can I do anything else for you before I go to find Mariel?"

"Sure. Walk away nice and slow so I can enjoy the view. You've got a great ass"

Heat crept into his face. *The woman was impossible.*

He hurried off to the kitchen, conscious of every step.

Mariel wasn't in the kitchen. She was in a bedroom off the hallway, helping a small boy pick up little white building blocks.

"There you are." He stood in the doorway. She sat on the floor, her legs tucked under her, holding open a cloth bag.

She looked up and her eyes softened. "Did you miss me?"

"I did." He meant it, too.

"Then sit down and help us. This is Nicky, Lindsay and Chris's son. They're leaving for Santa Marta tonight, and Nicky forgot to pack up his toys."

Zack sat cross-legged on the floor and helped scoop up the interlocking blocks. There were hundreds of them piled in one corner of the room.

"I like to build stuff," said Nicky. "My dad says I take after him."

A chuck wagon triangle pinged outside.

"Uh-oh, time to eat." Mariel smiled at Nicky. "You go on ahead. We'll finish this and come out in a minute."

"Thanks. I'm starving." He ran out the door and banged it shut.

"I hope your father doesn't come looking for us. He's going to think I lured you into an empty bedroom so I could have my wicked way with you." He waggled his eyebrows for effect.

"I rather think it's the other way around." She set

aside the bag and crawled over to where he was sitting. Still on her knees, she put her arms around his shoulders and pressed her lips into his neck. He closed his eyes and savored the sensations as lips moved from neck to the soft spot behind his ear. "Let's continue what we started last night," she whispered.

He was on fire, he couldn't think. He'd lain awake dreaming about her, tormenting himself with all the things he would do to her when he was finally exonerated and free to pursue her. She was bold and earthy and real, not the fragile flower her family made her out to be. He wanted her naked and hot, he wanted her legs wrapped around his body, her curves pressed into his chest. He wanted...

But not here.

He turned, brushed his mouth against hers, and pushed her gently away. "Your parents' house is not the place to do this, Mariel."

"I know. My mother's probably looking for me. She still thinks I'm a little kid."

As if on cue, the door flew open and an indignant woman glared at them both, her hands on her hips.

"Hi, Mama. We're about to finish in here."

"Is this him?"

"Zack...this is my mother, Francesca."

Zack glanced down to make sure he was presentable before getting to his feet and holding out his hand.

"Pleased to meet you."

She looked at his hand for a moment, then reluctantly shook it.

"The food's getting cold." She turned and wandered off.

He thought Mariel would look a bit remorseful, but instead she grinned. "Mama is old-fashioned, but her heart's in the right place." She hopped up and laced her fingers with his. "Shall we go?"

Zack allowed himself to be tugged out to the backyard, where the smell of barbecue greeted them.

He'd filled his plate for the second time when his phone buzzed in his back pocket. Pulling it out, he saw that it was the station. Excusing himself, he moved over to the side yard where he had some privacy.

"Leoni."

It was his training officer.

"What's up?"

"Your case."

A sick feeling washed over him. He leaned against the house, his heart thumped in his chest. "Did the wife change her mind?"

How could she do this? Everything had been going so well. He'd actually believed there would be an end to the misery of the last few weeks.

"Worse. She's disappeared."

"Oh, my God, did her husband kill her?"

"Get real."

"I'm serious. The guy's a lunatic."

"He's not the one who reported her missing. Her sister did. Wherever she is, she's definitely not coming in tomorrow."

Shoulders hunched, Zack ended the call and started back toward the barbecue. He could hear people laughing. Someone was singing. He stopped. Facing people would require more acting ability than he could manage. He changed direction and headed out to the street. It was rude to walk out without saying goodbye, but he couldn't face Mariel. When he got to the car he'd text her.

Sam's right. He couldn't continue to see her. It wouldn't be fair. She deserves someone who has a future.

Right now mine is in the toilet.

Chapter 13

The best proof of love is trust.
--Joyce Brothers

One hundred and eighty yesses and a dozen more maybes signed up for the fund-raiser at fifty dollars a ticket. That would fill the winery and its gardens, and, based on the well-known names, Mariel thought they'd get some good bids for the items to be auctioned.

She counted the number of gourmet dinners, wine lots, the baskets from merchants, and the gift certificates from various spas. Collectively they should bring in a few thousand dollars more to help the family.

The Callahan fund-raiser was a few days away, and she would be working that night. Maybe she'd ask Zack to come. He was a cop, but that shouldn't be awkward. He was one of the good guys.

Mariel's blood boiled every time she thought about

Michael. She'd forgotten to ask Zack if he knew the guy who'd put the poor kid in the hospital, not that he'd tell her. Identities of cops in trouble were a closely held secret.

Even though her father had taught her not to make judgments until you had all the facts, the local medial made it hard not to be angry. Maybe she *would* ask Zack...if he ever called her again.

After Saturday's barbecue, she thought he'd show up and apologize in person for leaving so abruptly. His text had been brief. "Have to leave. Work."

She'd gone looking for him, but nobody had seen him. Paige had taken her aside and quizzed her about being with Zack. Her sisters probably felt sorry for her. She was waiting for someone to sigh and say, "Oh, Mariel."

In the kitchen, she'd finally cornered Sam. He warned her to back off. Zack was commitment-shy. He had a lot on his mind these days. But when she pressed him for details, he told her she asked too many questions.

She swallowed her disappointment and went back to her lists. Yesterday she even planned an outing, hoping Zack would show up on her doorstep in the morning. He didn't. Self-doubt had plagued her all day. He said he liked her...his actions told her he more than liked her. But he hadn't even called. By three o'clock she'd swallowed her pride and called him. It went to voicemail.

She hadn't told him about the fund-raiser, the last event before Lane went back to Los Angeles.

Maybe he thinks I don't need him anymore.

She worked through her morning, and in the afternoon she dropped by the hospital to check on Michael. He couldn't have visitors yet, but she knew one of the ICU nurses. She waited for her friend to take a break and they went to the cafeteria for coffee.

"I heard about the fund-raiser. I plan to be there."

"We've had lots of donations for the silent auction. I hope it's a success." Mariel looked at her friend. "How is he?"

"I think he'll come around. The swelling is down in his brain, and he's moved, like he's trying to wake up."

"I'm so glad. His parents must be relieved."

The nurse stirred her coffee without looking up. "It's strange, but his mother hasn't been around for a couple of days. And his father hovers like a bird of prey, waiting to swoop down and take him away the minute he wakes up. None of the nurses like him."

"That's odd."

"I heard the father say his wife had to go out of town on business. Would you leave if your child was in a coma? It doesn't make sense."

The conversation had been unsettling, and Mariel continued to think about it long after she returned to work. At the Teen Center, Michael had always been quiet and eager to please. She got to know him when she helped the kids at the Center put on a Cinco de Mayo party. She couldn't imagine anyone wanting to hurt him.

But someone had—someone who was supposed to uphold the law—and that made her furious.

The door to her office swung open and Lane stood there, his shirt open to the waist, a Stetson covering his trademark rumpled hair.

"Hi there, twinkle toes." He closed the door behind him, leering at her from across the room.

Great. Just what I need.

Frayed nerve endings twitched along her spine. "What are you doing here, Lane?"

"I hear you're looking for some high-end auction items for the fund-raiser you're putting together, and I want to contribute."

"I've got plenty of stuff, but thank you."

She knew she was taking the wrong approach. Lane Brody preferred women to adore him. If they didn't, it simply made him try harder.

"Now is that any way to treat an old…friend." He paused on the word as if he was going to use another word.

She sighed. She'd play his game and then get rid of him. Stretching her mouth into a fake smile, she sat behind her desk, grateful for the protection it provided. Lane was unpredictable. He might stay where he was, or he might try to kiss her…and claim it had been merely for old time's sake.

"What do you have?"

"I've got the prize of a lifetime, darlin'. A date with Lane Brody. How about that?"

Deliver me from egotistical jerks.

"Really? A date with you? That should bring in a few dollars."

"A few thousand, you mean."

No need to be unkind. "These aren't your groupies, Lane. They're ordinary folks who work for a living."

"And I don't? My series is in reruns now, but I'm almost finished shooting the next season. The Nielsen rating is pretty high."

It was a good prize if he didn't renege when the bidding ended too low. "You're being very charitable, Lane. But don't be surprised if the person who bids doesn't quite meet your minimum number."

He moved closer. "Didn't you know? Cohen's bringing a few guests. No charge for them, of course. But they'll bid. Now where do I sign up?"

She knew Mr. Cohen was coming, but she didn't say anything.

"Tell you what," she said. "I'll contact your publicist. You don't have to do a thing but show up."

He sauntered over to the front of her desk and planted his hands on top of it as he leaned forward. "You going to do any dancing at the party?"

"No. I'm in charge of the party. I'll be busy running the show."

"Too bad, I miss those little private dances you used to do for me. Hope your new boyfriend appreciates them. If not, you know where to find me."

Mariel could feel heat staining her cheeks and a retort burning her tongue, but at the last moment Jess popped through the door.

"Sorry. I thought you were alone."

Lane straightened and picked a piece of lint off his cuff. "Didn't know you were in the tasting room today."

She inched back to the door, looking like a treed fox. A wounded look marred her perfect face, but was covered quickly by a pasted-on smile. "Sure am, sweetie. Have you tasted our double gold merlot yet?"

"Bought a case yesterday."

"Nice seeing you. Come find me when you're not so busy, Mariel." Jess scooted out the door.

His eyes narrowed. "I wonder what's got her back up."

Mariel snorted and rolled her eyes mentally. "Can't imagine."

"I'm due on location. Have to go."

She let out a breath, resisting the urge to lock her

door. How could she have been so stupid as to think herself in love with him? No wonder her parents and cousins thought she needed protection...protection from herself.

The few weeks she had been the center of Lane's attention, she had also been the center of speculation. Who was the little nobody Lane had hooked up with? There were always photographers following them around. They had no privacy. Some people ate it up. She hated it.

Calming herself with a few deep breaths, she went back to work. Flowers...that was the last decision she had to make for the auction. Best to do it today.

Zack, where are you?

The phone rang and she picked it up. Heavy breathing. She held it away from her ear and rummaged around in her desk for the whistle she'd bought. It was a cheap plastic kid's whistle, but she blew as hard as she could.

Ha. Take that. She waited until the dial tone resumed and slammed the phone down. No longer afraid, she was angry that someone thought they could intimidate her with childish pranks. It wasn't the tailgater. This was a harasser. But who? And why?

She should call Zack and tell him she had another breather. He'd be proud of her. She'd used the whistle exactly the way he told her. The need to see Zack warred with her need to protect her heart. If he was cooling down their relationship, then it would seem like she was chasing him, and if he rejected her, she'd be crushed again.

Indecisiveness had never been her problem. Instead, she forged ahead, sometimes too quickly, and she knew she was going to do it again.

So what if he says no?

He picked up on the first ring, startling her. "I was about to call you. Sorry I flaked on you Saturday. Like I said, it was work."

Air rushed out of her lungs and she held the phone tightly to her ear. "Everyone wondered what happened to you." She paused, but he didn't say any more. "I thought maybe you'd come by yesterday. I called. Did you get the message?"

"Yeah, I got it."

An awkward silence followed. Mariel plunged ahead. "I had another breather."

"Damn, I thought he'd gone away." The concern in his voice made her feel better. Maybe he still cared…at least a little. "I did what you told me to do. I blew a whistle."

"Good girl. Did he hang up?"

"Yes. I'm not going to put up with any more of that crap. I've had enough."

"Whoever it is will fade into the background now,

you'll see. The whole point is to scare you. If you're not scared, you've defeated him. But if anything else happens, you let me know. The torn nightgown still bothers me. I don't know what to make of it."

It bothered her, too. New deadbolts secured her doors now.

The conversation was ending and Mariel panicked. "We're having a fund-raiser tomorrow night at the winery. I…I need my boyfriend to be there. Are you possibly available?"

"What's it about?"

"It's for Michael Callahan. The kid who was beat up by the…"

He interrupted. "I know who he is."

"Can you come?"

* * *

He wanted to say, "Are you out of your mind, do you know who you are talking to?" but he couldn't, because nobody on the outside knew he was the one accused. He'd violated department policy by telling Sam, but telling Sam was like telling a post. He'd never rat him out.

Now he was going to hurt Mariel again. She was the best thing that had come into his life, but he had to say no. And it killed him.

He chose his words as carefully as he could. "You're the event planner at the winery. You're going to be a little busy. Sure you need me?"

"Lane's going to be there." She hesitated. "It's the last time. But if you don't want to come, don't."

The problem was he did want to come. But a fund-raiser for the Callahan kid?

"Is the father going to be there?" She might think it an odd question, but he had to know.

"This is put on by the owners of our winery and the charity that runs the Teen Center where Michael and his friends hang out after school. I heard the father never leaves Michael's bedside."

What could go wrong? If someone recognized him as a deputy, they might ask some unanswerable questions, but nobody knew he was the accused. And if the press found out later that he'd attended, it might actually show he had a compassionate side. He would maintain his innocence until he died. An innocent person might choose to show up at an auction to help a kid in need.

He was probably going to regret this, especially if his lawyer found out. But Mariel needed him.

"I'm free tomorrow night. What time do you want me there?

* * *

Mariel scanned the room, pleased with the results. Men in sport coats and women in cocktail dresses migrated between the banquet room and the outdoor gardens. The weather was perfect. June gloom in the morning had burned off, and the light purple grape clusters were already showing on the sun-warmed vines. Long tables with silent auction lots lined the walls, leaving the area in the center open. Businesses had been generous, and by the look of the bid sheets, the event was going to be a great success.

A trio played in the background, and the food tables were piled high with gourmet cheeses, delicate canapés made of crab and shrimp and other delicacies that were wine country trademarks. Everything was perfect.

Except Zack hadn't come.

She tamped down her disappointment and moved among the guests. Maybe she was too eager, or had misread his intentions when they sat on the floor in Nicky's room gathering up the blocks. She'd been the one to come on to him, but he certainly hadn't resisted the idea, only the location.

And then there was the night of the picnic. A one-night stand? Maybe for him, but not for her.

She spotted Lane in the center of a group of women, holding court. Running back and forth between the banquet room and the kitchen had kept her out of sight. Everything was handled now, and he kept looking at her, as if surprised she hadn't joined the group of adoring fans.

Jess hadn't joined it either. She was working behind the bar tonight, but anyone who knew her could read the jealous disapproval in her face. Now that Mariel was out of the picture, she'd convinced herself Lane would find his way back to her. Mariel knew they'd met after work for drinks a few times. It was obvious she was still not over him.

Jess could be difficult, but she was her best friend. Mariel was worried about her.

"You look like a woman who could use a glass of wine." The soft, rumbly voice next to her ear made her shiver with pleasure.

He came.

She turned around and took a full glass from his hand, reaching up on tiptoes to kiss him on the cheek. Tonight he wore a sport coat and slacks, his hair was slightly tousled, and his blue eyes were sleepy. "You clean up real good, deputy."

She expected him to smile. Instead he leaned next to her ear. "Shh…let's not spoil the event for the guests who aren't thrilled with cops right now."

He was right. The event was for Michael Callahan.

Lane looked her way and frowned. He laughed at something one of his admirers said and sauntered over. "I see your bodyguard's here."

"I go where she goes," said Zack.

Lane ignored him. "Sure wish you were dancing tonight, twinkle toes. Your sexy moves make a man wish he had a bed handy."

She wanted to smack him. "I'm working."

Lane cocked his head toward Zack. "Have you seen her dance?"

"I have. She and my sister did a jazz dance in a talent show their freshman year of high school. It was… unforgettable."

Mariel burst out laughing, her hand over her mouth. Zack sure had a way of reducing tension. She and Keira had pranced around to the Pink Panther theme in pink leotards with little pink ears pinned to their hair and whiskers painted on their faces. During a vigorous spin, their tails had fallen off. It had been a disaster.

"I can't believe you remember that."

"Let's see." He sipped from his glass, his eyes never leaving hers. "You both were barefoot and wore pink toenail polish, and at the end of the dance, you and Keira were as pink as your outfits."

"We were embarrassed. We'd tacked the tails on at the last minute and when they fell off, they left a gaping hole. It took me a long time before I could dance again in public."

They stared at each other and her heart did a tap dance. She heard Lane huffing off and the tinkling of silverware against glass plates. Someone laughed and another person clapped. But she was only aware of Zack, whose soft gaze was firmly settled on her mouth. Unconsciously she licked her lips and his mouth inched toward hers.

A voice called out from across the room. "Mariel. We need you over here."

He straightened and sipped from his glass, the mood broken.

She grinned at Zack and ran her fingers along his stubbly cheek. "Don't disappear again."

"Not a chance."

The auction was about to start. She hated leaving Zack, but it was a work night for her, and she had bid sheets to collect and a script to hand to the master of ceremonies. The highlight of the night was coming up…the announcement of the winner of the date with Lane Brody.

His ego must be bursting. He'd managed to get two pages of bids, each one greater than the last, although she hadn't identified the winner. Each bidder had a number.

Jess was supposed to help her gather the sheets, but she was nowhere in sight.

"Do you need help?"

"Here you are, always when I need you." She handed Zack a stack of papers. "Take them over to the table by the door."

"Always glad to be of service."

She put her hand on his arm. They'd raised a lot of money tonight, and she was being given the credit. The promotion was finally within reach. She'd burst if she didn't tell someone, but she only wanted to tell Zack.

"Did you know there might be a promotion in my future? It's not a done deal, but my manager said a lot was riding on this event, and it looks like I hit this one out of the park. I'm so excited I could do a little happy dance right here."

A stricken look passed over his face before he nodded. She must have imagined it.

"It's definitely a success." He leaned closer to her ear. "So what's this promotion?"

"It's technically in marketing. I'd still be doing winery-sponsored events, but in places all over the country. Isn't it exciting?"

The microphone squeaked a few times, but she'd hired a technician for the night to make sure there were no equipment failures. One of the winery's owners took the mike from the emcee, thanked everyone, said a few words about Michael and the Teen Center, and picked up the special heart-shaped bid sheet to announce the name of the person who'd won the date.

"And our big winner tonight is...well, this is a surprise...it's one of our employees."

Mariel's throat closed. Had someone written in her bid number? Oh, my God, she'd never even thought to look.

"Jessica Williams."

Jess? What is she doing? And how can she afford the two-thousand-dollar bid?

Her relief at not being put in a precarious position was quickly replaced by confusion. Why was Jess doing this to herself? She was merely prolonging her misery.

Mariel saw her standing next to the stage, a triumphant look on her face. Lane scowled, but the applause must have reminded him what his duties were. He took the microphone and grinned at Jess. "One of my favorites here at the winery. How lucky can I get? Congratulations, Jess."

Mariel looked around for Zack and saw him walking toward her. "What was that all about?"

"Not sure. Jess is still hurt over Lane's rejection. She refuses to believe he's an egotistical jerk. She thinks she can get him back." Zack wasn't paying attention. His eyes were focused on a man who'd just walked into the room.

She followed his gaze and saw a trim muscular man in a suit and tie marching toward the stage. He said a few words to the emcee, who stepped back up on the portable stage.

"Ladies and gentlemen. I'd like to introduce you to Michael's father, who will give us an update on his condition."

Well this was a turn of events she hadn't foreseen. Mariel watched the man stumble forward. Was he drunk? She put her hand out to ask Zack, but found nothing but air. Where had he gone? She turned around, expecting to see him at the bar or the food table. He wasn't standing by a door. What happened to him?

Her attention was back to the man on the stage. He said Michael was improving, and tomorrow the scumbag who'd done this to his boy would be revealed. The sheriff's department was holding a press conference to provide an update on the case. He invited everyone to show up at the county courthouse to demand answers and to support Michael.

"We need to weed out the bad cops who give the good ones a bad name."

The event ended and the crowd thinned. Zack was gone.

She shrugged and went back to work. As soon as the last person left, the cleanup crew would begin and she could go home. She wanted to talk to Jess, but her friend was as elusive as Zack tonight.

Did I say something? Why does he do this?

She stopped by her office to pick up her coat and purse. Her cell phone had no message. Irritation turned to anger.

Traffic was light on the road over to Napa and up to St. Helena. It took her less than an hour to get home. She drove into her carport and a man stepped out of the shadows. She almost   screamed as her heart leapt into her throat.

It was Zack.

"I have something to tell you."

Chapter 14

*The only true test of loyalty is fidelity in
the face of ruin and despair.*
--Eric Felton

Sam was right. He was an ass. He wasn't good enough
to be in the same room with her, let alone touch that
silky skin or taste those tempting lips. She felt
something for him. He could see it in her eyes. Maybe
it was infatuation or simply lust. Whatever it was, he
had to bring her back to reality and he knew the fall
would hurt both of them.

He was a man about to become unemployed, a man
who would be flayed in the media, and worst of all, a
man who might be charged with a crime he didn't
commit. If Mariel stood with him, as he was sure she
would, she'd be tainted. She'd lose her promotion and
her family's hard-earned respect, and it would be his

fault…again.

"Sorry, I didn't mean to scare you." He held the door open for her as she got out.

"Where did you go? One minute you were there and the next minute you were gone." Her tone of voice pierced him. He deserved it.

"I know. I'm sorry."

She unlocked the front door and turned on the lights. He stood by the couch while she tossed her coat on a chair and carried a large bag into the kitchen. She was wearing that black lacy dress she had on the night she turned into his driveway, but she'd taken off her shoes. She looked vulnerable in her bare feet.

God, he didn't want to hurt her.

"I brought home one of the unfinished bottles of merlot. It will go bad if someone doesn't drink it. I'm having a glass. You want one?"

"Sure. Didn't get to finish mine."

She poured and brought the glasses over, setting them on the coffee table next to a bowl of heart-shaped chocolate pieces. Tucking her legs under her, she curled up on the opposite side of the couch, as though distance would protect her.

He sipped slowly, letting the subtle cherry flavors slide down his throat. He remembered the last time he was here, and how he felt when the warm, trusting girl sitting across from him sat in his lap. She'd tasted of merlot and chocolate then. She would taste the same now.

Her eyes narrowed as she licked a drip from the side of her glass, her pink tongue darting around the edge to stop it. He swore under his breath when she set the glass down and stretched her arms over her head, arching her back. She must be exhausted after working all day and half the night.

"Back sore?"

"I've got a crick in my neck."

He moved over to the middle of the couch. "Turn around."

He moved her hair aside and worked his thumbs into her neck, then kneading her neck and shoulders. She sighed as the tension drained away. There were better ways to help her relax, but he wasn't here to seduce her.

This wasn't getting any easier, and he'd better get to it. The results of the independent investigation were being released tomorrow, but the name of the accused officer was supposed to be held in confidence. Too often names were leaked to the press. He wanted her to hear it from him…just in case.

He dropped his hands and turned her back around so he could face her.

"Like I said, I have something to tell you."

Her eyes widened. "Sounds serious."

By the time this was all over, she might hate him.

He'd been surprised to hear that her promotion was riding on the success of the fundraiser. She'd done a hell of a job. But if people found out about their relationship, her promotion—her job even—might be as dead as his own prospects.

She'd be devastated if that happened. It meant so much to her. And he'd be the cause of her pain.

"Can I ask you a question first?" She leaned forward to pick up her glass, giving him a beautiful view of her cleavage. Little sparks danced along his nerve endings, settling in an uncomfortable spot.

Sipping her wine, she gazed at him over the rim of her glass. The color of the wine, a deep red, sparkled in the crystal wineglass, catching light from the lamp behind her.

"Why did you run off tonight without saying anything? You did it at the barbecue, too. You said it was work, but I thought you said you were on vacation. It's annoying, Zack."

"Actually, it's rude."

"Then why did you do it?"

She leaned forward again, adjusting her ankles and squirming into the pillow behind her to get more comfortable. Distracted he felt himself reacting to her sexy movements. If she didn't stop, he'd lose control and be on top of her in two seconds.

He couldn't do that.

"Callahan came in. I thought it best if he didn't see me."

She paused and tilted her head, a frown line between her eyes.

"Because you're a cop? How would he know unless you've arrested him?" She chewed her lower lip as if working through a puzzle. She reached over and popped a chocolate in her mouth. "*Have* you arrested him?"

"Yes."

"So you left so he wouldn't see you and make a scene. I guess I can forgive you for that. I guess he isn't too fond of the sheriff's department right now with his child in the hospital."

"No, he isn't."

She stopped chewing and frowned, peering into her glass as if it were a crystal ball with all her answers.

"What about the barbecue?"

"I got a call. It had to do with Mrs. Callahan. She's disappeared."

"So that explains why she hasn't been to the hospital." She looked down, as if considering the impact of his words. "I went there to check on Michael and a nurse told me his mother hadn't been around for a few days."

He couldn't believe she'd gone to the hospital. This was getting worse by the minute. Next she'd be telling him she was Michael's babysitter.

He brought the conversation back. "Mrs. Callahan

witnessed Michael's injury. She made a statement initially that supported her husband's version of events. She was coming in to recant it. She never showed."

"Really? I hadn't heard that."

"Nobody has. It was privileged information."

She frowned, her eyebrows narrowing. "Okay, but what does this have to do with you? Why would any of this make you leave a party without telling me?"

He squeezed the edge of his shirt. "It has a lot to do with me."

"How?" She paused and looked down. "I shouldn't ask, but do you know the cop who did this, Zack?"

He'd been waiting for the question, and when it came, it hit him in the gut, even though he knew it was coming. Her feet were on the floor now, and she was scooting over toward him. If she touched him, he'd have to get up and walk away. Her eyes were huge as she searched his face, as if waiting for his answer.

"Yes, I know him. And I swear to you, Mariel, he didn't touch Michael."

She put her hand on his arm and he closed his eyes, hating what he had to say.

"Is he a friend, then? Someone you're close to? You're a loyal guy, Zack. Maybe you're letting friendship get in the way of common sense. Maybe that's what he said happened."

Then she cupped his face, her fingers soft as she

parted her lips and inched slowly toward him. "I can't stay mad at you, Zack. I was upset because you keep running away without telling me. Sometimes I think you don't like me. Then I remember the beautiful picnic and I know I'm wrong."

She was so close he could almost hear her heart beating. He closed the gap and kissed her open-mouthed, wrapping his arms around her and feeling the softness of her breasts against his chest. Chocolate melted into merlot as the kissed deepened and he let himself drift into a cloud of sensuality. He would regret this, but it might be the last time he'd touch her, taste her, feel her heart beating in rhythm with his own.

But he couldn't allow himself more than this one mind-searing kiss.

Breathless, he pulled away and put distance between them. Hopelessness weighed him down, but he couldn't wait any longer. He wanted her with a fierceness that scared him, but she deserved so much more than he could ever give.

Her voice wavered. "You're going to do it again, aren't you Zack? You're going to leave me."

"I have to, Mariel."

"Why? What have I done?" Her eyes filled with tears, and he couldn't stand to see her cry. "Is it because I'm not as smart as Lindsay and Paige, or the women you work with? Is that it?"

She felt inferior? My God, how could that be? "I can't believe you said that. You've got business instincts that make everything you touch successful. Your smile draws people to you. You're more than a party planner, Mariel. You're a magnet, and your winery knows it, and that's why you'll get your promotion." His shoulders slumped.

If I don't screw it up for her.

"Then what's this about?"

"It isn't you. It's me."

He didn't want to see her face, but only a coward would turn his back. So he looked into her eyes, wishing to God he didn't have to say the words.

"I'm the one, Mariel. I'm the one the media says put Michael Callahan in a coma."

* * *

Mariel couldn't breathe. She put her palm over her mouth and shook her head in denial as he walked toward the door.

"No."

"Yes. And it's not over. That's why we have to stop seeing each other."

"But..."

"If the truth doesn't come out and things go bad, I don't want you to be smeared, too. Think about your promotion. If I'm out of the picture, you can always say you booted me out as soon as you found out."

This wasn't what she was expecting. Zack couldn't be

the one. He'd never hurt anyone. He was the one who rescued animals and took care of his sister. He was the one who fought off the bullies for her in high school and came to her aid when she needed help discouraging Lane.

A child? Zack would never hurt a child. It wasn't in him to do such a thing.

And now he was leaving her…to *protect her*.

She wanted to speak, but the words wouldn't come. I *know you can't be the one*. Why couldn't she just say it? Why was her throat closing?

His hand was on the doorknob. "Callahan's attorney says I have PTSD and that the department is at fault for not sending me to a shrink when I returned. He says I lost it."

His shoulders shook. "I did not touch Michael. I called for backup the minute I saw him. I did punch Callahan to the floor to keep him from choking his wife to death. I'm not a monster. I don't have PTSD. I'm an act-first-ask-questions-later guy who can't seem to follow procedure. That's my flaw. You have to believe me."

She scrambled to her feet, but he'd already walked out of her house. The motorcycle engine revved. She listened until the sound faded away.

An old nursery rhyme flew into her head. *Sticks and stones can break my bones, but words can never hurt me.* It was bull. Every bone, muscle, and nerve ending in her body cried out in pain.

He'd come here tonight to end the charade and to make sure she knew there could be no more. He hadn't waited for a response. He expected her to be stunned or worse. *He thought I wouldn't believe him.*

Tomorrow was the press conference Callahan had touted. Tomorrow everyone might know Zack was the accused…her family, her friends at work, her boss. They would look at her and say, "Oh Mariel, poor Mariel, always making bad decisions. She was the one who organized the fund-raiser. Didn't she know her *boyfriend* was accused of the crime?"

Poor, naïve, trusting Mariel.

They'd say those things because they didn't know him…not like she did.

The dress was too tight. She went into her bedroom and took it off, along with her underwear. Slipping on a pair of tights and sweatshirt, she punched in her favorite Romero Brothers album on her phone and started to sway to the music. Closing her eyes, she let the sounds drift around her like gossamer threads blown in the wind. She filled her senses with the rhythms of the classical guitars while letting her body move of its own free will. Music was her escape. She used it like others used painkillers.

After a few minutes, she was calm enough to rinse

the glasses and think about what she could do. She'd go to the press conference. She'd stand up for her man.

There would be plenty of humiliation, but, by God, she'd suck it up. If she lost her promotion, so be it.

She was stronger now. She could do this.

He said he was innocent. She believed him, and not the media reports. And she had to make sure he knew she believed him.

Her thoughts turned to Paige's ex-boyfriend, a man who became reckless and violent after he'd returned from a combat zone. Could Zack have done this and not known it?

No. Never.

She stepped in the shower and washed away her uncertainty. Her hero wasn't perfect. No one was perfect. But he would never, ever hurt a defenseless boy.

He needed someone in his corner.

She wouldn't let him down.

Chapter 15

"I don't like to give up on people when they need someone not to give up on them."

— *Carroll Bryant*

The afternoon was scorching hot, but not as hot as the crowd milling around the entrance to the courthouse. Zack loosened his tie and pointed out a parking place to his attorney. Jonah had insisted on driving and, hell, Zack didn't care. It gave him time to ponder his fate without distractions.

They turned a corner and the crowd disappeared from view. A few media vans were present, but Zack hadn't noticed any signs or banners. He still couldn't believe Callahan would get this kind of turnout. Except for a few of the usual anti-cop protestors, most of the people must be here for the kid.

Zack got out of the car and went into one of the side doors of the building. The room where he and Jonah would wait was on the second floor. After going through the metal detector, they took the elevator up while Jonah filled him in on today's agenda. First they would hear the results of the independent investigation. Then they would meet with the District Attorney's representative to see if there was enough evidence for a trial.

"Remember, Zack, Callahan hasn't filed charges against you personally. He's filed against the department —the deeper pocket."

"Well, that's damn generous, isn't it?" Zack scowled and let the sarcasm flow.

"You aren't off the hook. If the investigation finds you at fault, the DA could still file criminal charges against you. But the department is solidly in your corner. They believe you, Zack."

"And none of this matters in the court of public opinion. The media has found me guilty. The only witness has disappeared. And the boy isn't awake yet."

Jonah looked at him and stopped outside the door. "Let's dump the attitude." He shoved open the door and they went inside.

Two people sat in metal folding chairs around a conference table After introductions were made, the assistant district attorney spoke, outlining various scenarios depending on what was in the final report.

"What about the investigation? I thought it been concluded?" He was curious, because he expected a half dozen people, including a couple of uniforms to be in the room. The Sheriff should have been there to make an official statement to the press, along with representatives from the Napa Police Department, who had performed the independent investigation.

"We expected to present results today," said the DA. "But there's been a change."

"Have you found Mrs. Callahan?"

"No, but the investigators are following a few leads. It seems she's been in a half dozen women's shelters in the Bay Area over the years. Not all the shelters require names. The team has a few more to check out."

"Is that it?" Zack settled back in his chair, waiting for the DA to finish.

"No, there's one other new development. Michael Callahan has regained consciousness. His doctors are very optimistic he'll make a full recovery."

Zack put his hands on the table in front of him. If this nightmare would soon go away, what were they doing here? Why were they still going through this initial step? Surely they'd talked to the kid.

Jonah glanced at him, then back at the DA. "That's great, but I sense a problem."

"He hasn't said a word since he woke up."

Zack gritted his teeth. It didn't mean he *wouldn't* speak. Michael might not be ready, especially if his mother was missing and his father was camped out next to his bed.

"The investigation won't be complete until the team speaks to the victim. We'll notify you when you need to come back in."

Zack shrugged. The news wasn't great, but he could wait. "There's a crowd outside, waiting for an announcement."

"We'll tell them the investigation is continuing. You can leave."

Zack and Jonah made their way through the corridors and chose to take the stairs to the lower floor. It was a mistake. A group of reporters stood outside, cameras ready.

"Don't look at them. They won't know who you are until the report's released."

They'd almost made it to the car when a voice he knew all too well shouted from the corner of the building. "That's the one. That's the guy who nearly killed my son."

Reporters crowded around. Zack tried to open the door, but someone held it closed. He took a deep breath and fought the urge to lash out. He heard Jonah saying "no comment" several times and finally got his hand on the door. Wrenching it open, he pushed a reporter aside and got in. Sweltering heat engulfed him from the closed car, but he dared not roll down the window.

He closed his ears to the taunts coming from some in the crowd, and stared straight ahead while Jonah inched his way forward, careful not to run anyone down. He wanted to shout his innocence and point his finger at the real perpetrator, but in the frenzy nobody would believe him.

"Take it easy. We're almost free." His attorney's voice was soothing, but it did nothing to quiet the agitation he felt. Had Mariel believed him? She's the only one he cared about. He hadn't waited around to find out when he left her condo last night.

They rounded a corner and stopped briefly at a stop sign. As they accelerated, Zack turned to look at a small group standing in front of the courthouse. Two men carried signs with slogans that should have made him angry. But it was the girl next to them who riveted his attention, a girl with haunted eyes.

Mariel was here?

He wanted to crawl into a hole and never come out.

The car lurched and pulled away. He didn't have the heart to look back.

* * *

The wall was hard, but if she didn't lean against something she'd slide to the ground. She had no business being here. Most of these people were strangers. But loyalty compelled her to stay.

A camera crew drove by. She turned into the wall, not wanting to be noticed. She'd hated being followed and photographed when she dated Lane. Pictures she hadn't known about popped up all over the Internet. It had been embarrassing and she never wanted go through anything like that again.

The crowd migrated to the courthouse steps. She kept to the edges so she could easily leave. An increase in noise level drew her attention. A man stood in front of a podium and read a statement. She was still too far away to hear, but the crowd roared. Voices screamed, "coverup" and "whitewash," and the mood turned angry. Obscenities felt like stones hitting her mind and body. She tried to back away, but someone called her name and she stopped.

Michael's father caught up to her and grabbed her arm. "Hey, aren't you the one who organized the party at the winery? I want you to say a few words. You must be as mad as the rest of us about this so-called delayed report. They're covering up for that dirty cop. Come on, you only need to say a few words." His palms were sweaty as he tugged at her arm. She shook it free.

"No. I don't have anything to say."

"Come on, babe. You're exactly what we need up there to keep these folks stirred up."

She was mortified. She had to get away.

"Let her go. She's not going to help you." It was Jess at her elbow, coming to her rescue. Thank God.

"Why not?"

"Because the "dirty cop" you identified for us earlier is her boyfriend."

Callahan looked at Mariel like she was an alien from another planet. "Is that true?"

She was trapped. Others crowded around her. She couldn't breathe. She'd always been pampered and protected. But there wasn't anyone to protect her now. She had to rely on herself. She could acknowledge her relationship with Zack and face the consequences, or she could deny it and be free of this suffocating crowd.

She swallowed and put up her hands as if to ward off blows. Somehow she found the courage she needed.

"I've known Zack Leoni most of my life, and he would never do what you say he did." She spit out the words, her breaths coming fast. "He's a kind, caring man. He'd never hurt a child."

"Bullshit." Callahan stepped in front of her and grabbed her. His beefy hands bit into her upper arms. "He beat up Michael and he punched me in the face. I've still got the bruise to prove it."

The crowd moved in. Angry sounds pelted her ears. She twisted and turned, then remembered what Zack had taught her. As soon as she went limp, Callahan let go, and she slid to the ground. The crowd moved back, far enough for her to scramble to her feet.

She pushed her way to the edge and sprinted to her car, Jess right behind her.

Mariel turned to face her. "What has gotten into you? Why did you tell them he's my boyfriend?"

Jess scowled and looked down, unable to meet her eyes. "I just told the truth."

"He's a good man, Jess. He doesn't deserve this. But he's not my boyfriend, even though I wanted it to be true. He came over to my house last night and told me he couldn't see me anymore."

She looked up. "Someone actually dumped you, huh? About time."

"Don't start. I can't take it right now."

She slammed her car door and drove off, checking her rear view mirror to make sure no one was following. She saw Jess with a smirk on her face. Confused, she almost went back, but she was an emotional mess. Her imagination was in overdrive.

There was only one person she wanted to see right now, but he probably didn't want to see her. Too bad. She had to clear things up between them.

As she drove, a niggling suspicion began to take shape. It was an "ah-hah," moment completely out of the blue.

What a fool I've been.

Teeth gritted, she passed the turnoff to Zack's house

and headed toward Napa. Zack could wait.

This could not.

Chapter 16

The trust of the innocent is the liar's most useful tool.
--Stephen King

Mariel parked in the Oxbow Marketplace lot and willed herself to be calm. Her throat and shoulders were tight with anger. Why had Jess done it? They were friends...best friends.

Jess lived in an apartment nearby, but her little red sports car wasn't parked down the street. Mariel needed to calm herself and to think. She'd wait here until she saw Jess's car.

Mariel still wasn't sure why Jess had been at the press conference. She didn't know Zack was the accused cop until Callahan had fingered him. Maybe she wanted to show support for Michael, although Mariel was sure she'd never met him. Jess didn't volunteer at the Teen

Center except for the few times Mariel convinced her to help. And she wasn't an activist.

She did make use of opportunities. Maybe she thought word would get back to the owners if she attended the press conference. But that didn't make sense unless she, too, had applied for the marketing job.

And there she is.

Jess parked on the street and went into her apartment building. Mariel waited a few more minutes before following. Bright red anger blazed in her heart. She had to calm down or she would lose control. All the ugly pieces fit together now. How could she not have seen it before?

Because my family's right. I'm too trusting.

Mariel didn't call or even knock. The apartment door was unlocked, so she walked in.

The shower was running. Mariel sat down and idly picking up a magazine. Throwing it down on the coffee table, she stood and looked out the window. Summer tourists strolled on the sidewalk. Some carried colorful shopping bags. A few had cardboard three-packs containing bottles from one of the nearby tasting rooms.

She stiffened when a door opened in the hallway.

"Mariel. You startled me." Jess's hair was wet, and she wore shorts and a halter top.

"How long did you stay at the courthouse?" Mariel

tried to keep the anger out of her voice, but she was shaking with rage.

"I left when you did. There wasn't going to be any more news." She took a soda out of the refrigerator and popped the top. "You want one?"

"Why did you do it, Jess?"

She paused and cocked her head. "My, but we're a bit testy, aren't we? Why don't you sit down and tell me what this is all about?"

Mariel remained standing. "This is about Lane, isn't it?" It wasn't a question. She knew the answer.

"I don't know what you're talking about." Jess put her soda down.

"I think you do. I think you still blame me for Lane's abandonment. But you don't get it. He didn't want you. And for that matter, he didn't want me. He wanted attention, he wanted to be news, he wanted his picture in the magazines. You, me, and whoever came before and after us, were nothing more than conveniences. Means to an end."

"No." Jess narrowed her eyes and banged on the kitchen counter. "He loved me. He was going to marry me. Then you came along with that seductive little dance you did at the Christmas party, and that was it. End of Jess."

She stomped into the living room and stood in front of Mariel, fists clenched, eyes blazing. "You pretend to be little miss innocent, the girl everybody looks out for, but you know what you are, Mariel Reynoso? You're a slut. Lane and I are getting back to together. It took most of my savings, but, by God, it was worth it. We've got that date I won, and we're going to talk. And I know once he hears me out, he'll realize what a mistake he made and take me back."

"You're delusional Jess. He's probably thinking up ways to get out of it."

"You're saying that because you're jealous. Your hot boyfriend burned you, and you can't stand to see me happy."

"You had a bit of luck today when Callahan identified Zack, didn't you? It gave you one more opportunity to discredit me. But it gave me an opportunity too…to come to grips with my feelings and to do what's right. I stood up for him because I love him. He means more to me than the promotion or even my job. If you think Lane cares about you, great. But if you think either will make you happy, you're wrong. You can't be happy without friends and you've just lost this one."

Silence echoed throughout the room. Jess was breathing hard, but she'd had her say. Now she looked wary, like she'd gone too far and wished she could take back some of the words.

"Just leave, okay?"

Mariel wasn't ready to leave, because she'd finally

connected the dots and the picture they made was even uglier. Staring right into her friend's eyes, she said, "You are the stalker, aren't you?"

Jess laughed, but she didn't deny it.

"I'm not talking about the tailgater. I'm talking about breathing into the phone and the break-in at my apartment. That was you. I gave you a key to my place last year when I first moved in. In fact, I still have the key to this place that you gave me. I'd planned to use it today, but the door was unlocked."

She shrugged. "I meant to scare you, that's all. You're surrounded by family members who've made it their purpose in life to shield you. I wanted to punish you for taking Lane. Then I had the brilliant idea to go to your house and fix it so it looked like a break-in."

"That's a crime, Jess."

"No it isn't. I had a key. I took nothing...except that sexy lingerie Lane gave you. It tore me up when you showed it to me. You were laughing, saying you'd never wear something like that. I found it, shredded it and threw it in the wastebasket."

I have to get out of here.

Jess hurried after her. "You're not going to tell anyone about all this, are you? It was a joke."

"You're in for a world of hurt, Jess." She fished Jess's key out of her purse and threw it on the floor, slamming the door as she left.

She was emotionally drained. All she wanted to do was go home, crawl under her covers, and sleep, but she had one more place to go. Zack had told her he was afraid she'd hate him. Now she had the same fear. She knew he'd seen her at the courthouse. He'd think she didn't believe him.

She had to go to him.

* * *

She hadn't been on this road since the night she was stalked, but she drove its winding curves without hesitation, ignoring the tension vibrating in her body. She saw only two cars, both going in the opposite direction, and she peeked in her rear view mirror to make sure nobody was behind her.

Daylight was fading when she arrived at Zack's house, but no light glowed through the windows in front. She got out of her car and pounded on the door.

"Zack. Let me in. It's Mariel."

Silence closed in, warning her to leave. He'd had enough drama for the day. He needed peace. But if she left, she might lose her nerve. She beat on the door again.

"Damn it, Zack, let me in."

No answer.

The door was locked and the curtains drawn in the front windows so she picked her way carefully to the rear of the house and tried the back door. It, too, was locked. Making a complete circle, she stopped in front of the garage door and pressed her forehead against the window. The car was in its space, but the Harley was not.

He was gone.

And he doesn't know that I love him.

The weight of her anguish pulled her down into darkness. She sat on the front porch steps, her head in her hands. She'd never forget his face as he'd driven away after the press conference. He'd looked straight at her with clenched jaw and hard eyes. He must have seen the protest signs held by two men next to her. He must have thought the worst.

She doesn't believe me.

Her glazed eyes scanned the landscape around her. In the fading light it looked almost surreal. Splashes of deep blue blended into the branches of green pines, creating a blurred montage of color. She shook her head and pulled out her phone, swiping at tear-filled eyes. She'd sat for almost an hour. He wasn't coming home tonight.

Taking a deep breath, she punched in Sam's number.

"Hi. It's Mariel. Does Zack happen to be there?"

"No."

"Do you know where he is?"

"What's this about?"

Embarrassment fueled her hesitation. She was in for

an "oh Mariel" moment and deserved it. "I went to the courthouse today. The investigation was supposed to be finished and the report released."

"Geez, Mariel. You just go looking for trouble."

"No. I had to go. I…I wanted to support Zack and I wanted to know what the report said. But it's been postponed. I don't know why."

"Did you see him?"

"He was in a car with another man. It passed right by me and he looked out the window, right into my face. His eyes looked haunted…I think he was upset because I was there."

"Shit, he probably thinks you have the same opinion as the rest of the world. The media has not been kind. They never are."

"I care about him, Sam. I want this to go away, but I know it won't until Michael wakes up and tells what happened. And he will. I have a feeling it will be very soon."

Her cousin's tone softened. "You've fallen for the guy haven't you? And don't say I'm taking after Nana. It's pretty obvious. You've let your heart overrule your head, as usual. I saw it and I let it happen. I should have stepped in."

"No, I'm tired of people stepping in. I've done this all myself and I need to live with it or fix it." She stopped to swipe at her eyes that were filling again. "You and

Mama and my sisters are not responsible for me. I'm responsible. If you keep protecting me and advising me and trying to fight my fights for me, I'll never learn. All of you treat me like a child, and that has to stop or I'll never have any self-esteem. Do you understand?"

"Maybe. But you didn't call me to give me a lecture."

"No. I'm trying to find Zack. I'm sitting outside his house. He's not here. And I don't want to explain in a text. I want to see him in person."

Sam paused, as if trying to find words. "If it's any consolation, I think he has feelings for you, too. I've seen the way he looks at you, like you're Baccarat crystal and he's a piece of carnival glass. He doesn't think he can ever be good enough for you. Especially now."

Her stomach felt like it had a balloon inflating, pressing against her lungs. Had she ruined everything by going to the courthouse today? Maybe, just maybe, they'd have a chance to explore their feelings when the drama ended.

"If he shows up, will you let me know?"

"Sure, but I'm headed out of town this week. We'll talk when I get back." He paused. "Hang in there, cuz. This will right itself. He just needs time. You have to give him space."

She put away her phone and got into her car. Sam was right. She had to be patient. If Zack cared about her, he'd give her a chance to explain.

But patience wasn't her forte.

Chapter 17

Make the most of yourself by fanning the tiny inner sparks of possibility into flames of achievement.
--Golda Meir

The Harley purred as he took the hairpin turns of the coast highway north of Jenner. The wind brushed Zack's face and blew the tension off his shoulders. When he rode, peace surrounded him. He had to be careful not to close his eyes and drift off the road.

The day had not turned out as he'd expected. His future was still a question. Would he be cleared and would he have a job when he was? *God, he hated this waiting.*

Even six months ago the job had seemed to be the right one, but now he wasn't so sure. What he needed was to get away, to hear waves hitting the beach, to feel sand beneath his bare feet. So he'd packed his saddlebags, strapped his bedroll to the back of the bike, and taken off.

He finally reached the stretch of coast he was looking for, pulled off the road, and locked up his bike. Taking his backpack over to a pile of driftwood, he took out a bottle of water and slipped off his boots. Waves rolled onto the shore, a roar in his ears, blocking his thoughts. He sat in the sand watching spray bounce off the rocks and waited for sunset.

Last time he watched the sun dip below the horizon, Mariel was with him. Just thinking about her used to make him happy.

A rock weighted his gut. It was clear where she stood.

Forget her. It's over.

He wondered if she'd been promoted. Brody could have interfered, but Zack didn't think so. At the fundraiser he'd been checking out all the lovelies, looking for his next conquest. Their relationship ploy had worked. Mariel was finally off his radar.

He watched a bird run into the receding water, then scurry out before it got too deep. Was he like that? Did he make a commitment, then step back before it was too late to change his mind? No, he was solid. Once he made up his mind, he went for it.

Except for Mariel.

She'd been too young when he developed his first crush on her...his sister's little friend...the dancer. While she practically grew up in front of him, he was always too old. Four years is a big difference when your best friend is telling you to be a girl's big brother. Helping out at the talent show he discovered he still had feelings for her, but the timing was off.

He sipped his water and let the breeze ruffle his hair. What was he going to do about Mariel?

He knew what he wanted to do. He closed his eyes and pictured that sunny smile of hers that stretched all the way to her eyes, her way of walking almost on her toes, the way she concentrated when she talked to people, always watching their lips so she didn't miss a word.

His hand tightened around the water bottle.

He loved the softness of her hair and the smooth skin of her shoulders. He liked the way she nuzzled his neck and rubbed her cheek against the stubble on his face, and the scent of merlot that surrounded her after she'd been at the winery. Best of all, he loved the way she made him feel...like no one else existed for her.

He'd wanted her since the day she'd grabbed his arm and brazenly announced to Brody they were a couple. Mariel brought his fragmented parts together. She made him feel important. She made him feel whole. And he'd been starting to believe she might care about him the way he cared about her,

And yet she'd been at the press conference with a protest sign. It didn't make any sense.

So I'm a lousy judge of character.

Ignoring the stab of pain in his gut, he finished his water and shoved the bottle back into his pack. Rolling up his pants legs, he gazed out over the water and watched a distant fishing boat making its way down the coast. He walked down to the water's edge and let the sea brush his bare feet. In June the water was still too cold for swimming. It would be too cold even in August.

He stood there until the sun sank into the horizon. His friends told him if you looked real hard, you might see a green flash as it disappeared. He didn't see it, but he wasn't here to look for freaks of nature. He was here to make decisions about his life without interruptions. Before tomorrow, that's what he was going to do.

A flock of seagulls squealed overhead, dipping into the water, looking for dinner, reminding him he was hungry. He walked far enough back so the water wouldn't reach him and unrolled his sleeping bag. Taking a couple of protein bars out of his bag, he sat on the sleeping bag and watched the sky turn from blue to black. It was a long time before he crawled inside and went to sleep, but when he did he was finally at peace.

The right decision had been in front of him all along.

He was the kind of guy who wanted to make a difference in the world, even if it was one person at a time. He was a protector, a saver. He didn't like being under a public microscope, but visibility came with the job. While he liked doing things his own way, his tour in Afghanistan had taught him he could be part of a team.

He wanted to keep his career and he wanted to be the best. He'd fight hard to keep it, even if he had to change.

Stars were bright overhead, but by morning the fog would be in. He opened the sleeping bag and crawled in.

* * *

Zack woke up to the sun in his face. He'd slept a long time, the ebb and flow of the surf in his ears. The air was damp, but he was warm in his cocoon. Pleased with the decisions he made the night before, he packed up his gear and loaded it on his bike. On his way home he'd grab a coffee and a breakfast roll at the convenience store he passed yesterday.

Sam would be gone for a few days. His house was available. Zack needed a change of scenery. It would be a good place to hide out until he heard from his attorney.

If he didn't go stir crazy.

* * *

Restless days dragged into sleepless nights. On advice of counsel, Zack stayed out of sight. Nobody tried to camp on his doorstep, as his attorney had feared. He'd gone home to pick up clothes and hadn't seen anyone lurking nearby.

His self-enforced confinement grated. Grace Callahan hadn't been located. Michael was awake, but hadn't spoken. Zack's future still hung like a twig on a dying tree.

On an impulse, he opened his laptop and scrolled through the known shelters in the Bay Area. He knew the ones in Napa, Sonoma, and Marin counties had been contacted, but there were several in San Francisco and Oakland. Where to start? Maybe she hadn't gone to a shelter. Maybe she was hiding at a friend's house.

But you don't know who her friends are.

He closed the laptop and headed for the carport.

Jumping on the Harley, he roared out of Sam's drive and headed for the hills on the east side of Napa Valley. His thoughts turned to Mariel. No texts or messages. She'd definitely given up on him. Fine. He'd didn't want someone who didn't trust him, who didn't believe in him, who thought he was tainted like the rest of the world did.

And yet a text from Sam had given him pause. Don't write her off. Get your shit together, then talk to her.

Talking might be a good idea.

If he could ditch the pain he felt at her betrayal.

Today he was on a different quest. He hoped it panned out. If not, he might as well resign and save the department the embarrassment.

Although he'd had to turn in his gun and his badge, pending the results of the investigation, he still had his identification card. And he still had access to work files on his laptop.

Grace Callahan's sister was the one who'd reported her missing. She lived off the Silverado Trail. Maybe she could give him some leads. If anyone knew who Grace's friends were, it would be her sister.

If she doesn't run screaming when she opens her door.

It was a chance he had to take. Sitting idle while others determined his fate was not his idea of time well spent except he would be breaking rules again...big time.

The homes in this area were built on hillsides. Names and numbers on mailboxes at street level identified the occupants. The first set of numbers was too low. He'd have to ride for several miles to get into the range he needed.

His attorney would have a fit if he knew what he was doing. Hell, his training officer, who was in his corner one hundred percent, would ream him, too. Looking for this witness violated all kinds of procedures. But he'd always been a risk-taker, and this one was worth it. If anyone believed in his innocence, it would be Grace Callahan's sister. Family members generally knew what went on, though they often didn't know what to do about it.

A mailbox nestled between two oaks had the right numbers, and the wrought iron gate next to it stood open. It was a sign, an invitation to follow his instincts.

A sign? Now I'm thinking like Nana Reynoso.

He parked the bike a little off to the side, not wanting to advertise his presence until he'd practiced what he would say. It wouldn't do to stroll up and blatantly announce that he was the cop who was accused of knocking out her nephew. And by the way, he didn't do it, but he did flatten her douchebag brother-in-law.

No, he had to be careful. He didn't want to scare her. He'd be in even more trouble if he did.

The woman who answered the door seemed cautious, but she didn't slam the door in his face. She knew who he was—who didn't, these days—and she stood quietly, waiting for him to speak.

"I'm sorry to bother you, ma'am, but I hoped you might be willing to talk to me."

Her eyes narrowed through the screen door. "What about?"

"I'm looking for your sister. I'd like to talk to some of her friends. Maybe they know where she might be."

"Are you back on the job?"

"No, ma'am."

"Then why are you here?"

This was harder than he thought, but something was off. She wasn't the least bit afraid of him, and that could only mean one thing. He was right.

"You know I'm innocent, don't you?"

She hesitated, then opened the door, her gaze never leaving his face. "Come in."

He followed her to a sunny kitchen at the back of the house. The windows faced a well-tended garden with grape vines on the hill beyond. Tall sunflowers lined one side of the yard, framing a green lawn.

"Nice yard. Are you the one who takes care of it?"

"It's my pride and joy." Her pleased expression quickly faded. "Coffee?"

They took their mugs outside and sat on a bench.

"I know your sister's taken refuge in a shelter for battered women in the past. Do you think she's in one now?"

The woman sipped her coffee. "When her husband drinks, he gets nasty. When he sobers up he's horrified and sorry and tells her he'll never hit her again." She shook her head. "The fool believes him. She loves him. She's sure he'll change."

His shoulders slumped. He'd heard this so often. Plus, he'd seen it happen in his own family. His aunt was a victim of spousal abuse. When he tried to figure out what had prompted his instant, uncharacteristic response toward Callahan, he was sure he'd reacted because of his aunt.

He shook his head. "It's a common story, I'm sorry to say."

"Well this time there's a difference. This time the bastard hit Michael." She finished her coffee and stood.

It was gratifying to hear that someone believed him. But it was hearsay. She couldn't testify on his behalf. She wasn't there.

"You've talked to your sister? She knows Michael is going to recover?"

The woman leaned down and pulled a weed, shaking dirt from the roots. "Yes. It's a miracle. God's hand was in it for sure."

"But she's staying away."

She stared at him, her hands on her hips, the cup dangling from her finger. "Do you blame her? She's afraid. She's afraid for her son, too. But she has to figure things out before she shows up at the hospital. She wants to take Michael, but her husband has influential friends. He'd never allow it."

"Grace isn't alone. She has you. And she has the law on her side, if she will testify against him. In this state she can, you know."

"She wants to see Michael. It's killing her that she

can't."

"I think Michael is waiting for her, too. He's hasn't talked. Not one word. Did you know that?"

Her eyes widened. "No, I didn't. I haven't been able to see him. Only the parents can visit him in ICU."

"Can you tell me where she is? The detective would like to talk to her."

"It's not up to me."

It was time to leave. He wasn't going to get any more information from this woman. She was loyal to her sister and would protect her.

His only hope was that the evidence at the scene somehow proved his innocence.

Or maybe Michael would finally speak.

He rose and extended his hand. "Thank you for your time. If you think of anything that might help, please call me." He handed her a card with his cell phone number written on the back.

He didn't re-enter the house, but strode around the side toward the place he'd left his bike. He put on his helmet and climbed on, waiting for the heaviness in his chest to subside. What had he expected? An address? The fact that the woman knew he hadn't hurt her nephew was comforting, but it wouldn't help.

Grace Callahan had to come forward.

He hoped she figured things out in time.

The key turned and he engaged the starter. The

engine roared to life. As he turned the bike toward the road, a woman came running out of the house.

"Wait."

He'd only seen her once, but he never forgot a face, even one with a bruise that was starting to turn yellow.

He turned off the engine and followed her back into the house.

Grace gripped his hand while she told her story. It was not easy to hear. Zack wanted to prompt her when she faltered, but knew his role was to simply listen. At the end, she agreed to make a formal statement if Zack promised to help her get a restraining order. Her sister promised to go with her.

She wanted to see Michael, but was afraid of her husband.

Zack called the station and arranged for a deputy to meet her at the hospital. As much as he'd love to be there for the reunion, his job was done. Others would take over now. He could breathe a little easier.

One worry would be crossed off the list. Others remained.

At least he would be exonerated. A great surge of relief rolled through him. He still had decisions to make, but first he had to get through his disciplinary hearing.

It was scheduled for the day after tomorrow. Tonight he would concentrate on getting a good night's sleep.

After tomorrow he'd start making plans.

* * *

The sheriff's administrative offices were next to the courthouse. No crowds milled around today. Employees rushed between buildings and potential jurists lined up in front of a security checkpoint, waiting to be cleared to enter their courtrooms. He found the building he was looking for and was ushered into a small office with only one person inside.

Zack expected the hearing officer to be formal. Instead, he shook his hand, gestured him to a seat, inquired about his family, and told an old cop joke. If it was a technique to make him relax, it worked. Feeling like a deflating balloon, Zack leaned against the chair back and willed his fingers to rest easy on his knees as he slowly released air from his lungs.

He hadn't brought his attorney. Whatever the decision was, he'd accept it without argument or use of the county's appeal process. This was one-on-one. He'd screwed up, and he'd take his lumps.

"I understand you have cause to celebrate. The brutality charges filed against the department have been dropped."

"Yes, sir."

When Michael's mother was reunited with her son, they had both told the detectives the truth. Fear, not trauma, had kept the boy from talking. He'd been terrified that his mother would be harmed if he spoke out.

So he'd kept quiet.

Now Zack wanted to put the entire mess behind him. The official report would be released tomorrow. Callahan had been arrested. There'd be no chance of an out-of-court settlement now, so he dropped his suit. His wife was filing for divorce and had agreed to testify against him during his trial.

The actions he'd taken when he found Michael on the floor had been correct and Grace Callahan had corroborated his story. His reputation, however, was still tarnished. Cops had a hard time overcoming a false charge, even when cleared.

"But we still have this other matter." The officer got up and moved to the chair next to Zack's. "You've been written up a few times by your supervisor for handling situations your way, not ours. You seem to have a problem following the rules, Deputy Leoni. Care to explain that to me?"

Zack hadn't prepared a speech, nor had he expected to say anything in his defense. Probationary employees were just that…they served at the will of the employer for an entire year in this county. While respecting the system, his responses had been pure reaction on a couple of occasions. The disciplinary letters in his file were the penalties. Too many, and you were suddenly a liability.

And you were let go.

"I have no excuse for my action toward Callahan. The man did not respond to my commands. He continued to attack his wife, so I did what I had to do to protect the victim." He looked straight into the face of the hearing officer. "I pulled him off and slugged him. It stunned him long enough for me to subdue him."

It was risky, but he had done what seemed necessary at the time. He'd come from a war zone. Mulling over various courses of actions before making a decision sometimes cost lives. In the military it was called necessary use of force.

And then there was the flash of memory from his childhood—his aunt taking abuse while he stood by and couldn't do anything about it. It had only happened in his presence once, but it had been imbedded in his memory forever.

The officer returned to the chair behind his desk and wrote something on a piece of paper.

"Normally, I would recommend termination of employment after so many other violations. Fortunately, most were minor. In this case you had other alternatives which were appropriate and which you did not take. If the suspect did not respond to your initial commands, you could have pulled out your baton or even your weapon. Even in situations of high emotion, most people will respond to authority." He looked down at the paper in front of him. "I understand the perpetrator was inebriated and enraged. That makes your job more difficult."

"It does, sir."

He paused and steepled his fingers in front of him. "In so many other ways, you are a good employee and I think by the time you complete your field training you'll be an excellent one. I've spent considerable time reviewing your file, talking to your training officer, your coworkers and your immediate supervisors. They all say you have the makings of a good officer. So I'm going to give you a break. I'm going to recommend a full week off, this time without pay, and some retraining in the area of subduing a violent suspect. I'm also going to extend your probation. You'll be watched carefully. No more screw ups."

He looked up, waiting for a response.

Zack swallowed. This was the best possible outcome. He should get up, say thank you, and walk out. But he suddenly had more to say.

"It isn't easy to transition back into civilian life after serving overseas. I don't know how many other guys in the department have been called back to serve while working here—probably a lot a few years back—but when it happens, they may need a little help. Sounds like this organization is willing to work with them."

"We try." He handed Zack a folder with a written evaluation. "I've put you back on the duty roster."

"Thank you." He shook the lieutenant's hand and walked out the door, feeling lighter than he had in a very long time.

The conclusion was totally unexpected. He thought he'd be spending the afternoon cleaning out his locker at the substation.

He had a future again.

Chapter 18

Trust your instinct to the end, though
you can render no reason.
--Ralph Waldo Emerson

Mariel stared at the boxes scattered across the floor. The condo lease was up in a week and she'd decided not to renew. She'd narrowed her choices to two apartments available in downtown Sonoma, both closer to work. But she had to admit she'd miss looking out her window and seeing the vineyards that surrounded her place in St. Helena.

"Are you taking these or donating them?" Mama held up a pair of candlesticks.

"Donating." Jess had given them to her. She'd never liked them, anyway.

Mama worked quietly, wrapping dishes in newspapers before fitting them into a box. "I still think you should move back home. Apartments in downtown Sonoma are expensive."

"I appreciate the offer, but we've been through this. Sonoma is closer than Napa to my winery. I can live on the Plaza and walk to coffee houses and a grocery store. The Tuesday farmer's market is right across the street. And when I need my family, I'll be equidistant from you on the Napa side of the hills and Paige on the Sonoma side."

"You're right. It's perfect for you."

Mariel's jaw dropped. "I am?"

Mama set the heavy box aside, taped the lid and picked up an empty one. "You need people around you, Mariel. After all that happened, Papa and I think you shouldn't be alone."

Neither did she but Zack hadn't called. Her lip quivered, but she bit down hard.

She picked up a stack of newspapers her grandmother had saved for her, using the sheets of paper to wrap crystal wine glasses. A headline on the front page of one grabbed her attention. It was the story describing Michael's recovery and his mother's corroborating statements. She already knew Callahan's charges had been dropped because Sam had told her.

The roller coaster Zack had been on was finally slowing.

Her long-stemmed wine goblets required two sheets

of paper, and she methodically wrapped all six and put them in the box. They were her favorites…beautiful, delicate, and shaped perfectly for her winery's merlot. Memory flashed of the night Zack had waited for her to come home from the fund-raiser. She hadn't been fired, as Zack had feared. She suspected her relationship with Zack's hadn't even been on her employer's radar.

The promotion was hers. The formal offer was made yesterday after a lengthy interview. If she accepted, they would begin training her in November when tourist season ended.

"Have you heard anything from Zack?"

Mind-reading seemed to be one of her mother's talents and she wasn't even a blood relative of Nana Reynoso's. "I was just thinking about him. How did you know?"

"You get this sad, faraway look on your face, like when you were little and wanted to take home all the kittens and puppies at the animal shelter." Mama paused and tilted her head. "Why don't you go see him? Find out if he's all right."

Mariel placed a wrapped crystal goblet in a box and stared at her mother. "You think I should visit Zack?"

"I know how miserable you are. Find out once and for all where you stand. The old impulsive Mariel would have done it. The new one is more cautious." She picked up the tape and stretched out a piece to secure a lid. "You've changed. You weigh choices before you make decisions. You think things through. You plan ahead now. But Papa and I want you to be happy. You won't be until you talk to Zack and make him understand you believed in him."

Mariel narrowed her eyes. "You've been talking to Sam, haven't you?"

"Sam and your grandmother. Nana Reynoso says Zack is a good man. She might act crazy sometimes, but she's a shrewd judge of character. She never liked Jess, you know. She said the day she met her, a jay with gorgeous blue wings, fluttered and pranced on the hood of her car and left a nasty pile when it flew off. It was a sign."

Laughter rolled around in Mariel's stomach until it burst out in a loud, unladylike whoop. When she could control herself, she gave her mother a hug. "Where does Nana get these pronouncements? Papa never makes any."

"Your grandmother is a unique woman. Never doubt it. She's the bane of my existence, but I love her dearly."

They finished their packing for the day and Mama left. Mariel bathed and changed and picked up her notebook. La Golondrina was co-sponsoring the annual talent show in Napa this year, donating wines to be sold at intermission to enhance the proceeds. As usual, the talent show beneficiary was the library.

After her humiliation five years ago, Mariel had refused to attend any other shows, although she dutifully bought a ticket every year. This year she'd be front and center.

Suppressing a shudder, she methodically checked off each task. Tickets for the door were in her car. Wines had been delivered to the auditorium. Cartons of clean glasses from the party rental company should be stacked behind the serving tables by now. A low flower arrangement had been ordered for the appetizer table and should be on its way.

A local cheese maker had donated wheels of cheddar and dry jack to be served with delicate crackers, all arranged on plates with olives, dried cranberries and nuts.

The food and wine would be perfectly paired.

Leaving the mess in her apartment, she showered and changed and headed for Napa. The road that went to Zack's house was around the next turn. The longing to see him was agonizing. Did she dare?

The old Mariel wouldn't have hesitated.

She veered sharply to the right and headed up into the hills.

* * *

She pounded on the door. It seemed like yesterday she had done the same thing. But this time he was definitely home.

"Go away."

"I won't go until I talk to you."

"I don't want to talk to you."

"Yes you do, Zack Leoni. Open the door."

The door abruptly widened and Mariel rushed in before he changed his mind.

"What are you doing here, Mariel?" His tone blistered her. "Didn't you hear everything at the press conference?" He strode past her and turned down the music. She heard Kenny Chesney in the background.

"Sit down, Leoni."

His lip curled. "You're ordering me around now?"

"Yes. Sit down." She pointed at the couch.

He sat. His gaze seemed to follow her as she paced. She sifted her fingers through her hair and stood in front of him. "I've been thinking."

"That must be something new."

She glared. "Don't be an asshole."

He looked down. "Sorry. I've had a rough month."

She took the time to study his face. His eyes were steady despite the fine lines crisscrossed at the corners. His chin was firm and his jaw stiff, although covered with about two days of stubble. His hair had grown out a bit and curled around his ears. He actually looked more relaxed than the last time she'd seen him, but her visit was definitely not welcome.

She sat down beside him and took his hand, not

letting him pull away. "I know you saw me at the courthouse. I wasn't there because I supported the protestors. I went there to make sure someone was in your corner."

"You had a sign."

"No, I happened to be standing next to two men with signs. You know me. Have I ever been political? I go to work like everyone else. I do the best job I can. I come home, and if there's time, I dance or teach kids to dance."

His brows drew together. "If you say so."

She wasn't getting through to him. His emotional barriers were raised high. After all he'd been through, what had she expected? She softened her voice. "Are you all right?"

"I'll survive. But I'm glad it's over."

"Do you want to tell me what happened that day."

"No. I want to bury it. It's over. I've let it go."

He dropped her hand, got up and walked over to the fireplace. Getting down on his knees, he stacked kindling around the wood, as if to be ready for the cooler temperatures of the night.

He placed a log carefully onto the pile of kindling. It was too warm to light a fire yet. His focus turned back to her. He rose, but he didn't sit back down beside her.

"Tell me why you are really here." His tone was angry.

"Have you talked to Sam?"

"Sam isn't my keeper and despite what you think, we don't have a conversation every day."

She swallowed, but her gaze held his. "I knew in my heart that you didn't do what they said you did. You couldn't. Even as a teenager, you had integrity and compassion. I should have said that the night you came to my house. I should have told you I believe you."

He folded his arms. "It hurt when you didn't. I thought you trusted me."

"You left too soon. I was still trying to absorb what you said."

She jumped up and stood in front of him. "I do trust you. In fact, I think I'm a little bit in love with you." There. She said it. Let him chew on that one for awhile.

He stepped back, not quite hiding the hunger in his eyes. "It's too late for us, Mariel."

"No it isn't." The old Mariel was in charge, the spontaneous, impulsive Mariel who made snap decisions and shrugged off consequences. Zack loved her...she could feel it...and she wasn't going to let him get away.

"I think you should go now."

She folded her own arms and stood her ground. "Is that what you really want? I don't think so." He had to make the next move, or all was lost.

They stood toe to toe, looking into each other's eyes. He dropped his arms, hesitated, then reached over and wrapped them around her. She could feel him shudder. "I need you Mariel. I wake up to an empty bed, wishing you were beside me. I sit in my kitchen and I imagine you dancing between the stove and the sink, a sexy smile on your face, the one you reserve for me. And I know my life is empty without you. I love you. Only you. Always you."

She sighed against his solid shoulder and felt his arms tighten. The only sound was a rustling in the trees outside an open window.

After that beautiful outpouring, she wasn't a little bit in love. Her whole heart was involved. She wanted to stay in Zack's arms forever, she wanted to hear his heart beneath her ear, and breathe in his spicy scent. She wanted to hear that special sound he made when he pleasured her, and feel his body nestled against her when she woke up in the night.

She knew it wasn't enough for her to want these things. He had to want them, too.

And he did. So where did that leave them?

* * *

Zack felt every swell and curve of her body as he held her close. When she said she was a little bit in love with him the ice around it started to melt. He wanted nothing more than to lead her into the bedroom and make love to her until she cried out in release, over and over again. This kind, generous, lovable girl had always deserved so much more than what he could give her. But maybe they had a chance.

But you're still on probation. Are you sure you can pass this time?

He could feel her heart beating against his own and her quickened breathing when he pulled her against him. Her lips were sweet and suggestive. It was agony not to kiss her, but if he did, there'd be more. And there could not be more. Not yet.

His hold tightened and he heard her sigh. She felt so good in his arms. He buried his nose in her fragrant hair and rubbed his cheek against its softness. If he could only stay like this for a while, he might be able to chase away the tensions of the past month. But even now he was responding to her, and he would have to release her soon or else throw all his scruples out the window and let himself be lost in the comfort of her words and her body.

He wanted to marry her, but he couldn't ask her until he knew he could change, until he knew he had a real career, until all the bad publicity was in the past. Callahan's trial would raise it all again and he didn't want her to be dragged into the middle of it. She needed her new job to prove to herself she'd made it in the work world, that she was every bit as successful as her sisters were. Her promotion was her big chance. He didn't want to spoil it for her.

He loosened his hold and stepped back to look at her face. Her expression was serene. She'd grown up. And she'd lost some of her carefree spirit. He hoped not all of it.

"Love is important Zack. Knowing you love me makes so much difference. But we've barely gotten to know each other again. I sense you need time to be sure you're not reacting to the pressures you've faced."

She opened the front door and paused. "We both have a lot to process. Now that we've cleared the air, I feel so much better. Thank you, Zack."

"For what?"

"For believing in *me*. For helping me see what's important in life. You helped me sort through some serious stuff. My family loves me, but they can't live my life for me. And you can be sure I'll be more careful about my friends."

"Your friends?"

"Jess. She was my stalker. She was jealous. She's also delusional. Lane won't take her back." Her eyes softened. "Jealousy is a powerful emotion but so is love. When you're ready, come to me. I'll be waiting."

She smiled and closed the door behind her.

Chapter 19

Trust in dreams, for in them is hidden
the gate to eternity.
--Khalil Gibran

Mariel was late and she didn't care. Clouds couldn't have been softer than the air she walked on. Zack loved her. It was a start.

She arrived at the auditorium and found a parking place near the stage door. Performers scurried around backstage, putting on makeup, adjusting costumes. She heard a few nervous giggles. Heat stained her cheeks when she remembered with fierce clarity her own preparations five years ago and the fiasco that followed.

Thank God I'm not dancing.

Waving at Sam backstage, she skirted the aisle and went to the front of the building. Enlarged book covers made into posters lined the walls.

People were already in line outside, and when the doors opened, and many would rush to the refreshment table. Her critical eye spotted a drooping stem in the centerpiece and she pulled it out before lining up the glasses that were now set out on the table. Four volunteers from the Friends of the Library stood ready to pour.

Everything was ready.

Soft music piped in over the intercom while the doors opened. Mariel stiffened. It was the same music that greeted people the year she'd been scheduled to dance. Did they use the same music every year? She swallowed and nodded as pleasantly as she could at people she knew. Her parents would be there, but she hadn't seen them yet. Paige was coming with her friend Sarah.

Don't be silly. Nobody will remember your debacle.

People continued to file in, going to their seats, or milling around the entryway, sipping wine and nibbling on cheese. Mariel answered questions about the wines and handed out brochures. When the lights dimmed, she took cartons of used glasses to the kitchen and made sure there were bottles opened for the intermission. Plenty of food left.

The show started, and Mariel slipped into the back of the auditorium to watch three of her dance students perform a modern routine they'd choreographed. At the end she clapped while the house lights came up, as if she was the proud mama of all three.

"Hey, there."

Her stomach fluttered and her breath caught. Zack was here.

She turned and smiled, not sure what to say.

He picked up her hand and twined his fingers through hers. "Come backstage with me for a minute."

She hesitated. "Why?"

"Sam called. Said he needed help. I don't want him to think I've disappeared."

"I'm in charge of the refreshments."

"Everything's under control. Come on." He tugged at her hand, and she sighed. If he wanted to be with her, she'd go. She'd been afraid of losing him for so long it was nice to know they were a couple. Weren't they?

They went out the front and skirted the edge of the building, heading for a stage door. It was a perfect summer evening with a gentle breeze. He stopped outside the door and pulled her into his arms.

His lips were as warm as his body, and Mariel groaned when the kiss deepened. He raised his head. "I've missed you." He trailed kisses down her neck.

She put her hands up against his cheeks and held his face. "You saw me a couple of hours ago."

"Too long."

"I have to get back. Maybe we can go somewhere after the show."

His eyebrows raised. "Are you propositioning me again?"

"Now there's a thought."

She felt every inch of him as he molded her to his body and took her mouth in another searing kiss that made her ache fiercely.

"Wait." She pulled back. "I forgot to ask. Did you lose your job?"

"No."

"Oh my God, that's wonderful."

His eyes softened. "It's going to be tough, but I think I can fit in."

"I know you can."

He grinned and tilted his head. "Sam told me you got your promotion. You've worked hard for it. Congrat…"

She interrupted. "What Sam doesn't know is I turned it down."

He gathered her close, and she melted into him, aware that she was holding her breath, waiting for his response.

"I can't let you do that."

She pulled back so she could look into his eyes. "It's not your decision, Zack. I'm making my own decisions now. I like my job here. If I stay, we can be together. I had planned to pursue you. Relentlessly. I'm not letting you get away."

His hands dug into her shoulders. "You have me. You don't have to give up your promotion."

The door banged open to reveal Sam standing inside. "Leoni? Get in here. It's time."

Zack guided Mariel into the back area of the stage where banks of lights and microphones hung down near chairs and props. No performers were there, but the house lights were dim, waiting for the next act.

They stood almost exactly in the same spot as four years before. Mariel glanced at the microphones, putting her fingers to her lips and pointing upward.

"What are shushing me for?"

"The microphones. Remember?"

"I do. And that's why we're standing here."

He pulled something out of his pocket and turned to face her. "Five years ago you wanted me and I turned you down...rudely."

"Zack! What are you doing?" She heard a buzz from the audience. A few people tittered.

"This time I'm asking *you*." He got down on one knee. "Mariel Reynoso, I love you. It's going to be tough for a while, but I think you're up for it. Will you marry me?"

No sound came from the floor of the auditorium. It was if everyone was waiting for her answer.

She expelled her breath and pulled him to his feet. Vibrating with excitement, she looked him straight in the eyes. "Yes. I'll marry you." She couldn't believe what was happening. He was turning one of the worst days of her life into one of the best.

Applause started, a few handclaps, followed by a roar from the audience. When the curtain opened, everyone was clapping. She saw Paige and Sarah standing. But the lights blinded her. Or maybe it was tears.

"Take a bow. You're on stage," Sam growled from the sidelines.

They walked to the middle of the stage and faced each other. Zack pulled a clunky class ring out of his pocket and slid it on her finger. It was too big, but she didn't care. She held up her hand and wiggled her fingers. More whistles and shouts greeted them.

"Okay. Get off the stage." Sam beckoned to them when the music for the next act started.

They ran behind the curtain and Sam gave her a quick hug. "Okay, cuz and cuz-to-be. Back to work, now."

Zack took her in his arms. "You won't have to give up your promotion. It's important to you. I can fend for myself when you're gone. We'll make this work somehow."

"No. I called the winery the minute I left your house. I told them I was turning it down. It's too late. You're stuck with me."

She closed her eyes and savored the man in her arms.

She could hardly wait to hear someone say, "Oh, Mariel…" Because the rest of the sentence would be "she's finally got something right."

She looked into his beloved face. "My promotion isn't important. The fact that I could earn it is. It will be better for me to remain at this winery, getting as much experience as I can. Because someday I want to start my own event planning business. Magic Moments with Mariel. How does that sound?

He laughed and hugged her. "Great, as long as most of your magic moments are with me."

They might have to put off getting married for a while, but it would happen. Knowing Zack, he'd want to be sure he passed probation.

For now, she'd get to plan an engagement party—a big, splashy, fabulous one—her own.

* * *

She might have known she wouldn't get to plan her own party. Paige and Lindsay insisted they'd do it, since she had planned parties for them both.

"You're the honoree. You need to relax and mingle and enjoy the attention." Paige sat on a stool in her new house, her laptop in front of her. "Sarah is going to cater —you know what a terrific cook she is—and your boss is donating all the wine for the party."

Mariel handed Paige a cup of tea and took one over to Lindsay, who sat on the couch with magazines open in front of her.

"I really wish you would let me do something. I feel so useless." And wasn't that part of the old Mariel... feeling invisible when her sisters were around? She sipped her tea, thought about how she would phrase her thoughts, and jumped up.

"Okay, this is very sweet, and I really appreciate what you're doing. But this is my area of expertise and I have to insist on having some input."

Paige shrugged. "You're right. Planning parties isn't our thing. But we want to do this for you. You're our little sister."

"Didn't you used to say 'annoying little sister?' "

"Did I?" Paige feigned an innocent look.

"I admit, my wedding was fabulous...and you planned every detail," said Lindsay. "If you want something, chime in. But Paige and I are paying for it. No argument."

"I can't let you do that."

"Sure you can," said Paige.

Mariel ran over and hugged each beloved sister in turn. Her party was going to be the best ever.

Chapter 20

All's well that ends well.
--William Shakespeare

They chose Zack's special hilltop for the party. A large white tent sheltered long tables with white cloths and red napkins. Single red roses in crystal vases were scattered throughout. Mariel wanted it to look simple and red was her color.

Dress was casual because of the season, and a shuttle bus, provided by Chris, brought guests up the hill from two winery parking lots below. A three-piece combo played soft jazz in the background…something for Mama. She was happy even though Mariel was moving in with Zack the day after the party. Papa had accepted the situation, knowing they'd be married by winter.

Mariel focused on her handsome fiancé. Dressed in slacks and a collared shirt, he was the consummate host…greeting guests, shaking hands, and leading them over to the beverage table. He looked relaxed and happy. Her insides melted with pride.

"Be careful or you'll start drooling." Nana Reynoso stood next to Mariel, her gaze focused on Zack. "I have to admit, he is drool-worthy. How'd you get so lucky?"

"Hmm, let's see. I closed my eyes, counted to three, and threw salt over my shoulder?"

"What?"

She laughed, hugging her grandmother. "I'm making it up. Don't you make up all those outrageous things you say?"

"Tut. Don't be insulting. I see, I interpret, I say. I'm a living oracle." She did a smooth moonwalk, ended in a twirl, and bowed. "At least that's what I always told your father and his brother Miguel. They scoffed, of course, but my girls were all believers. Still are."

"Papa is practical to the core. Sometimes I wonder if he's your son."

"He's asked me the same question, impertinent boy. I roll my eyes and point at my long dead husband's picture. Pedro is the image of his father."

"Hey." Zack strode up with a beer in his hand. He leaned down and kissed Nana on the cheek as he handed it to her.

"Ah, Zachary. You correctly predicted I was thirsty and I have a prediction for you."

"You do?" He cocked his head, all attention.

"Happiness, success, and lots of unissued tickets in your life."

Mariel interrupted. "Tickets?"

Nana stared up into the sky and closed her eyes as if meditating, then looked back at them. "Yes…those are the speeding tickets Zack isn't going to give me. I'll deserve every one—lead foot you know—but he won't catch me."

"Because you're fast."

"And cute. Don't forget cute."

"Sorry. No family deals," said Zack, giving her a hug. "And yes. You are definitely cute."

Nana preened and sashayed toward the beer keg.

He turned to Mariel. "Come on twinkle toes. It's time to get this party started."

She planted her hands on her hips. "Don't you dare call me that."

"Just teasing." He looked full of mischief, and Mariel's ire softened as she gazed at this gorgeous man who was finally hers. He leaned down and whispered in her ear. "But I am looking forward to a special little dance when we get home after the party…something that involves the removal of clothes?"

"You've got it, babe." Heat thrummed through her as she thought about what she would do to him later.

Their fingers twined as they made their way to the

tent where Sam was getting ready to announce dinner. Jake had flown in lobsters from Maine. She still couldn't believe it. Lobsters at her engagement party...as one of the main courses. They wouldn't be able to top that at the wedding.

Zack stopped. "Uh oh, look who walked in."

Mariel gazed out over the crowd, stopping on a blond head. It was Jess...an uninvited guest...making her way toward the bar.

"Shall I escort her back to the shuttle?"

"No." Mariel narrowed her eyes. "She looks miserable."

As predicted, Lane had wiggled out of the date with Jess and paid the amount of the bid himself. Last she heard, he was dating a member of his cast.

"Did you ever tell anyone what she did to you?"

Mariel shrugged. What was the point? In the end she was the one who was happy and Jess was no longer her friend. "No, but there were rumors, and rumors can be more hurtful than telling everyone the truth. I doubt if she's going to enjoy herself. She was probably embarrassed to be the only one of the winery employees not invited to the party and decided to crash."

Mariel turned away and smiled at Zack. Nothing could ruin her mood.

This was the best engagement party ever, and she was the star...she and the man who once turned her world upside down, and now would be by her side forever.

About the Author

Author of nine novels and eight history books, Pamela Gibson is a former City Manager who lives part time in Northern California's wine country and part time in the Nevada desert. Having spent the last three years messing about in boats, a hobby that included a five-thousand-mile trip in a 32-foot Nordic Tug with her patient spouse, she now spends most of her time indoors happily reading, writing, cooking and keeping up with the antics of her gran-cats, gran-dog, and gran-fish. Sadly, the gran-lizard went to his final reward. If you want to learn more about her activities go to https://www.pamelagibsonwrites.com and sign up for her quarterly newsletter. Or stalk her in these places:

Bookbub: www.bookbub.com/profile/pamela-gibson
Facebook: https://www.facebook.com/pages/Author-Pamela-Gibson/1557080444511057
Twitter: https://www.twitter.com/pamgibsonwrites
Goodreads: https://www.goodreads.com/pamgibsonwrites
Amazon: https://www.amazon.com/Pamela-Gibson/e/B00MKVB4XE

Novels by Pamela Gibson

Love in Wine Country Series

A Kiss of Cabernet
A Touch of Chardonnay
You Were Mine at Merlot
Sauvignon Blanc to Sigh For
A Pinot for Your Thoughts
It's a Zin to Tell a Lie (Fall 2018)

St. Helena Vineyard Series (Novellas)

Plumb Crazy About You
A Model of Perfection
The Christmas Angel

Historicals

Scandal's Child

Here's a sneak peek at the next book in the Love in Wine Country Series, Sauvignon Blanc to Sigh For

Chapter 1

"A friend is someone who understands your past, believes in your future, and accepts you just the way you are."
– Unknown

Something clattered against her bedroom window.

Sarah James sat bolt upright in bed, listening for a repeat of the strange sound.

It pinged again…this time unmistakable.

She slid from the bed and sidled over to the edge of the second story window. Slowly folding her fingers around the edge of the curtain, she peered outside.

A bulky male form stood under the window, clearly outlined by the streetlight.

"Crap."

She hurried downstairs, opened the front door, and scurried down the steps. The grass was wet under her bare feet, but she had to get to the side yard before her nosy neighbor woke up.

"Sam," she hissed. "Get your butt over here."

Thank God no cars drove by on her quiet street this time of night. Or was it morning? The front door stood open, and she strode through, not waiting for the man to follow.

Sam Reynoso, her friend since the sixth grade, flopped down on her big, overstuffed couch and dropped his head in his hands.

"Jen and I broke up."

Sarah stood over the giant in her plaid flannel pajamas, her hands on her hips. *So that's what this was all about.* She'd heard it before…about four times. Sam had a knack for hooking up with the wrong women.

"How did you get here? I didn't see your Harley."

"Walked."

"From Jen's house?"

"Oxbow Market."

"That's a good two miles away."

"Needed to clear my head. I downed a couple of shooters." He looked up at her through long-lashed honey-brown eyes. "Got any coffee?"

"I guess so." She glanced at the wall clock and headed for the kitchen. Whenever Sam had a problem with his love life, he showed up on her doorstep, expecting her to have ready- made answers, as if she were a female version of Dr. Phil. Some expert she was! Sarah barely remembered the last time *she* had a date. Oh, yeah, the goofy guy in the Finance Department who dressed up like Batman every Halloween.

She chose a strong blend and put it in the

coffeemaker. When it finished, she took the mug out to the living room and handed it to Sam.

"What's with the pebbles? You scared the crap out of me."

"I wasn't sure you'd hear me at the door, and I lost my cell."

"Again?"

He nodded.

"All right. Spill." Sarah sat on the chair opposite and folded her arms. She hoped this wasn't going to take all night. Planners for the City of Napa showed up for meetings on time, and she had one at eight o'clock.

"Everything was great." He ran his fingers through his dark hair, a mark of frustration Sarah had come to know. "We were talking about taking a vacation together. She wanted to go to Hawaii. I was up for that. You know I love to surf."

He put down his cup and stared into space. "Then she said she wanted to go to Europe. I said I wasn't sure if I could swing that, but I'd try if it would make her happy. Then she laughed. She said she didn't want a guy who made her happy. She wanted a guy who made her want, who made her beg, who made her earn everything she got from him. And that wasn't me. But she'd give me a chance to change. Change? She's the one who needs to change. I told her it was over. Then I walked out."

Sarah narrowed her eyes. "Good for you. You're better

off without her."

He looked up, his lopsided grin telling her he agreed. "I can't believe I stayed with her this long, Sarah."

"That's what you said about Taylor and Emily and Alyssa when you broke up with them." He didn't sound upset, or she wouldn't have brought up the names of the other girls he'd *thought* he was in love with and ended up dumping.

"What's wrong with me, Sarah?"

It was a valid question, but she wasn't sure she knew the answer. Sam was a control freak, and he'd blown a couple of his relationships because of it. When he met Jen, he tamped down his natural tendencies and let her take the lead. His personality change was amazing. Obviously, it had been a mistake. Jen must have needed someone more dominant. She would have liked the old Sam better.

"You love everyone, Sam. So you think everyone should love you back. And life isn't like that." She tucked her legs under her in the big chair. "The first time I met Jen, I pegged her as a woman with some heavy issues, so I'm glad she's gone. You deserve better."

He nodded and picked up his coffee.

Sarah yawned. "You can crash on the couch, and tomorrow I'll take you to get your bike. I have to get some sleep." She went upstairs and came back down with her extra pillow and a blanket.

He stood and leaned over to kiss her cheek. "Thanks, Sarah Bear. You're always here for me."

The use of his pet name for her made her smile. Sam would be okay…he always recovered from his breakups quickly.

She plodded back upstairs, fell into bed, and closed her eyes. She pictured Sam on her couch. With women he was like a puppy, bewildered and unhappy when they didn't live up to his expectations. He was a hot guy, over six feet tall, with a strong jaw and thick, dark hair worn longer in the front. He had well-developed muscles from lifting heavy wine barrels, and he wore his pants low on his hips. With his swagger and intensity, he reminded her of a sexy gunslinger in a Western movie.

Women seemed to gravitate toward him, as if he was sending out little magnetic currents of sex appeal, but lately, he'd attracted the wrong kind of woman. He had a weakness for redheads, and if one showed any interest in him, he was all over her. Jen had long, red hair, straight and slick, and had reeled him in by doing nothing more than crooking her little finger.

What he needed was someone solid and dependable, someone who appreciated his kind heart and his vulnerability. Someone like…

She couldn't keep her eyes open any longer. It was midnight. Her alarm would buzz in her ear around six. Plus, her workload was extra-heavy because her vacation was coming up.

If she could only get through the next week, she'd be finished with a major project and out the door. Her boss had already approved her time off. She could hardly wait.

* * *

Sam rolled over and caught himself before he fell off the narrow couch. What time was it? He kicked off the blanket and stretched. Damn Jen. What had he seen in her, anyway? Sarah was right. She was good for a few laughs, but she wasn't the one.

He wandered into Sarah's kitchen and refilled the coffee pot, checking out the offerings in the refrigerator. Sarah was a damn good cook and tried different recipes all the time, even when she was cooking only for herself. He lifted out a bowl and took off the foil cover. It was some kind of casserole with shrimp. Scooping up a hefty portion into a ceramic dish, he stuck it in the microwave.

"You're up. I thought I smelled coffee." Sarah, showered and dressed in a tailored skirt and high-necked blouse, wandered into the kitchen. Sam admired her fresh-scrubbed look. Her long, dark blond hair was tied back in a prim twist at the back of her neck, and her wire rim glasses made her blue eyes look huge. A soft, flowery scent wafted into the room with her.

The microwave beeped and Sam took out the bowl,

sticking a spoon in it. "What is this? It smells great." He took a bite and closed his eyes. God, the woman could cook.

"Shrimp and grits…a recipe from the South. I found it in an old cookbook in a used bookstore. I'm going to try she-crab soup next." Sarah poured her coffee and sliced a piece of banana bread she'd made the day before.

"Call me. I'll come over and help you eat it."

Cooking was Sarah's salvation. She worked long hours, and relaxed by concentrating on recipes, modifying them, making them her own. Her cooking fetish started when her parents divorced. They had both remarried and now lived out of state, but Sarah came back to Napa after working briefly in Southern California. It was the last place she'd had a real home, she once told him. It was where she belonged. She never wanted to move again.

He ate every bite of the shrimp dish, scraped the bowl clean, and set it in the sink. Funny how he felt so much at home in Sarah's little cottage. Thank God she wasn't married. He didn't know what he'd do when that day came. Even a tolerant husband wouldn't want his wife's male friends showing up in the middle of the night.

A shadow darkened his thoughts.

What would you have done if she'd married your brother,

Aiden? He definitely wouldn't have wanted you around.

He shrugged it off. Aiden's home was a tent in Africa, or a hut in South America, or a hotel room in some foreign hot spot, living wherever his news service sent him. It would never be in Napa, where Sarah wanted to be.

Sarah grabbed her keys and looked over her shoulder. "Come on. Leave the dish in the sink. I'll get it later. I can't be late this morning."

He gulped down his own coffee and followed her out to the one-car garage. Tall aspen trees were golden in the morning sunlight, and the brilliantly colored leaves of a red Japanese maple covered the ground next to the driveway. It was a glorious fall day in the Napa Valley, and tourists would soon be up and on their way to winery tasting rooms.

"I'll drop you at Oxbow Market so you can pick up your bike. Get in."

He slanted a glance at her while she drove. Sarah was in a good mood this morning. When she smiled, her skin crinkled at the corners of her eyes and her mouth turned up at the corners. He loved her smile. It made him warm all over. Wasn't that what friendship was all about? He could let down his defenses around Sarah, be himself, and know he would be accepted, even when his behavior left much to be desired.

Like showing up on her doorstep at midnight.

"Here's your stop."

He opened the door, and turned to her. "Thanks, Sarah Bear."

"Any time."

He saluted and watched until her car was out of sight.

* * *

Sarah breezed into her office and sat at her desk. Booting up her computer, she pulled a large file out of the drawer. She'd check her emails and then head over to the public works department for her meeting.

One was from Sam's cousin Paige. "Lunch today?"

She checked her calendar and wrote a response. "Sure. Meet you at noon at our usual place."

The meeting droned on all morning, and Sarah decided to walk the few blocks to the restaurant near the waterfront. Fresh air cleared her head, and she looked forward to spending time with Paige, her best female friend.

"Hey." Paige was already seated at an outdoor table overlooking the Napa River. Her hair was pulled back in a French braid and her eyes were bright with happiness.

Sarah ambled over and seated herself. "You look like you won the lottery. What's up?"

Paige beamed, her smile as broad as the river behind her. "We're adopting. Our request was approved."

"That's fabulous." Sarah came around the table and hugged her friend. She pictured Paige as a mother. She'd seen her pamper and nurture failing vineyards, coaxing them back into health with her special skills. She'd be a terrific mom.

A little twinge of jealousy threaded through her, but she shook it off. Paige and her husband, Jake, had been through a lot, and deserved to be happy.

A baby. Imagine.

Sarah sat back down and smiled. Although she and Paige had been close since elementary school, she knew in her heart Paige would soon be busy with her husband and child.

But I still have Sam.

The three of them were the same age, and had shared classes all through school.

While they ordered lunch, Paige filled her in on the details of the upcoming adoption. When she finished, she turned the conversation back to Sarah.

"Where are you going on your vacation?"

"I don't know. I was thinking about the beach. Maybe the Sonoma Coast. Lots of vacation rentals there, and it's not too cold yet. I want to be where I can take long walks and look at the ocean."

"Why don't you go to Aiden's apartment? Lindsay said it's quite nice, and he's still gone. It's in Santa Marta, right on the coast."

Sarah shook her head. "That would be awkward."

Aiden was handsome and charming—a real catch, if you liked the dark, brooding type. Sarah remembered how easily she'd fallen under his spell. But Sam's older brother was married to his career, and traveled to all parts of the world to write in-depth pieces about current issues for a popular news service. He knew she was a nester and had ended their fling.

She was over him, but a stay in his apartment might send a different message. As tempting as a week in Santa Marta might be, she'd have to pass.

Instead, she changed the subject. "So, did you hear? Sam broke up with Jen."

Paige shook her head. "Good. That woman was bad news. I don't know why he persists in hooking up with women in bars."

"Not just any women…redheads."

"I've never understood that."

Sarah stopped chewing. "Maybe it's an identity thing. He thinks people dismiss him because Aiden is a brilliant writer and is well known in his field, and big brother Antonio made a fortune in the software industry. Of the three, Sam's decided to be the macho brother. With a hot redhead on his arm, he gets lots of attention."

Paige nodded. "Good theory. He's a terrific winemaker, but as an amateur, he doesn't get much notice. I know he's a take-charge kind of guy and tends to go overboard, but he has a good heart. He's been working for Papa on weekends, trying to help him keep up with his paperwork."

Sarah smiled. "He's got so much to offer. I'm sure he'll find the right girl someday."

Paige cocked her head and narrowed her eyes, a sly smile on her lips. "He just needs to look in the right place."

Paige finished her lunch and swatted Sarah's hand away from the check. "I'll get this. You need to save your money for your vacation."

"You're sure? Thanks."

Paige tilted her head to one side. "Why don't you take a cruise or hop on a plane and go to one of those singles resorts? You need to do something un-Sarah, something on the wild side. You need to loosen up. Hook up with a hot guy."

Sarah wrinkled her nose. Paige loved to give her advice, and had never given up trying to fix her up with blind dates. "Right. That's exactly what I should do," she said with friendly sarcasm. "If I want to completely relax, I'd go to one of those cooking schools in France or Italy. But it's too late to do that now. Maybe next year."

Paige's eyes sparkled with mischief. "I'll consult Nana Reynoso. She'll close her eyes, pretend to meditate, and then make a pithy prediction about your future based on aching joints or the behavior of crows she saw on the back fence."

"No. Don't do that. Her predictions are often correct, and I don't want her telling me I'm destined to be single my entire life."

Nana Reynoso, the beloved, eccentric matriarch of Paige's family, had them all convinced she had "the sight," and often gave bizarre predictions about the future. Sarah was sure she made up most of them.

They walked out and hugged in the parking lot. Paige climbed into her old truck and waved. Sarah watched it turn into traffic and disappear. A weight lodged in her stomach. All of her friends were married or engaged. Some were mothers. Maybe Paige was right. She needed to do something different.

She plodded back to her office while mentally outlining her report, wondering in an always-running corner of her mind how Sam was today. She would have called him, but he hadn't had time to replace his lost phone.

Her own phone rang and she dug it out of her purse.

"It's me. My phone was at the bar."

"Were your ears burning? Paige and I had lunch and your name came up."

"Yeah? She can talk about something other than the soon-to-be-new member of her family?"

"That was the main topic." Sarah crossed the street

with the traffic light, her ear to the phone. "How are you feeling today?"

"Crappy. I need some of your cooking."

She laughed. Sam was good for her ego. He never allowed leftovers when he ate at her house.

"Okay. Come over about six thirty. I'll try that she-crab soup and make some hush puppies to go with it."

"I'm salivating all over this phone. I'll bring the wine."

"A light, fruity chardonnay if you have one. It should pair well."

"Great."

He paused as she reached the block where her office was located. "And Sarah, I need to talk to you about something."

"You haven't found a replacement for Jen, already have you?"

"It's not about my love life."

"Well, that's a relief. I'd have to serve sorbet for dessert to cool you down."

"It's serious. See you at six thirty."

He disconnected the call. Sarah looked at her phone and put it back in her purse as she entered her office building.

What was he up to now?